WOLVEN

WoL

VEN

BY DI TOFT

SCHOLASTIC INC.
NEW YORK TORONTO LONDON AUCKLAND
SYDNEY MEXICO CITY NEW DELHI HONG KONG

ISBN 978-0-545-25518-9

12 11 10 9 8 7 6 5 4 3 2 1   10 11 12 13 14 15/0

Printed in the U.S.A.   40
This edition first printing, September 2010

The text type was set in Lino Letter.
The display type was set in Marketing Script.
Book design by Phil Falco

CONTENTS

CHAPTER 1
HELD TO RANSOM

In Nat Carver's opinion, the strange animal being paraded before him looked as though it owed its origins more to Dr. Frankenstein than Mr. Darwin. For once he felt lost for words, although he could think of a few he might have said if his mum hadn't been there.

This, he thought, *has got to be a joke.*

But when the silence became prolonged and uncomfortable, the kind where no one really knows what to say for the best, Nat knew it was no joke.

Behind him, his granddad, Mick, forced air through his false teeth, making a humming noise like a kazoo, a clear sign that he didn't know what to say, either. "I'm flabbergasted," he muttered at last.

"It's a lot bigger than I thought it would be," whispered Nat's mum, also clearly stunned by the creature standing before them.

"And a heck of a lot older," muttered Mick, sharing some of Nat's dismay. He turned to the farmer.

"You're playing a prank, Alec," said Mick angrily. "Our Nat wants a pedigree puppy, not this scraggy ol' mutt."

Despite the wasted journey, Nat thought that it had been worth it just to meet this miserable old farmer. Alec Tate had enormous, ill-fitting false teeth and the type of lugubrious mug Nat normally associated with a bloodhound or getting your face squashed in the doors of an elevator.

Nat's mum, Jude, watched nervously from the safety of the barn door, in case the animal made any sudden move toward her. It kept blinking as though it wasn't used to the sunlight, and plunked its hindquarters down on the dusty ground, quietly ignoring its visitors. When it opened its vast mouth to yawn, Nat and his grandfather hastily stepped backward. They stared in fascination as the top of the dog's head appeared to become detached from the bottom half, revealing rows of sharp, white teeth. Then it made a loud noise like a supersonic jet taking off. Despite his initial disappointment, Nat found himself grinning.

Fed up with waiting for Tate to answer him, Mick tried again, hoping to lighten the awkward moment. "I mean, look at the beast. It's so big our Nat could ride the beggar home."

"Might not look like much at the moment," said Mr. Tate. "He's going through an adolescent phase. Looks a bit out of proportion."

You're so *not kidding,* Nat agreed silently.

Sensing his audience wasn't impressed, Alec Tate's bloodhound face reddened. His eyes flickered shiftily, as if he were trying to think of something to say to make the dog appear more attractive. Nat, who was not by nature an unreasonable person, tried to be fair. If you looked past the obvious odd parts—the crusty, sparse fur and the strong smell, which Nat imagined as squiggly stink lines rising upward from the strange-looking body like in a cartoon—it wasn't *that* bad.

His mum, who was not usually keen on things that bite, seemed to have recovered well after seeing all those teeth in just the one mouth. She came out from behind the barn door, reached out, and gingerly patted the too-big head.

"Hello, boy," she said softly.

Mr. Tate grinned for the first time, sensing a shift in opinion. When the sunlight hit his false teeth, the solar glare made black spots appear in front of Nat's eyes.

Mick knelt down to make friends with the dog. As his lanky body folded up, his knobbly knees popped loudly. Nat's grandfather was lofty and thin, and dressed in clothes you wouldn't usually expect to see on a person of his years. He had eight silver earrings in his left ear and a shaved head, usually covered by a hat. Today, to mark the special occasion of dog buying, he wore his favorite: a green velvet pillbox with tiny mirrors embroidered on it. His lack of head hair was compensated for by a long, wispy beard, which he normally wore in a braid. On *really* special occasions he had been known to dye it purple, and it was at those times, much to Nat's deep embarrassment, that his granddad could be found playing air guitar, or even worse, air *fiddle*.

"Is that *mange*?" Jude asked the farmer suspiciously, pointing to the crusty greenish patches that almost covered the dog's entire body.

"Mange?" exclaimed Mr. Tate, clearly insulted. "'Course

it ain't the *mange*! That's only a bit of dung. Show me a dog that don't like to have a roll in a cowpat now an' then, and I'll say it ain't no proper dog!"

Jude snatched her hand away in horror, wiping it hastily on her jeans.

"Why is it, exactly, that you're getting rid of him?" asked Mick.

"Er . . . he was the last in the litter," replied Mr. Tate, avoiding Mick's eyes.

Nat held out his hand to the dog, which until this moment had ignored him. It got up awkwardly and gave him a halfhearted lick, as though it thought it ought to make an effort.

"There you are—the boy's bonded with him already!" exclaimed Mr. Tate, giving them the benefit of his false teeth again.

Jude still looked doubtful; she knew that Nat had his heart set on a puppy, not a fully grown dog like this malodorous mongrel.

"Other 'uns were black and tan, and him being white, he's what they call a throwback—that's why he's going cheaplike."

"Thought dogs normally went *woof*, not *cheep*," said Mick, winking at Nat, who shot him a withering look.

A sudden realization hit Nat: *Mr. Tate is lying*. There was something about the farmer's manner that made him feel uneasy; his story didn't ring true. Something told Nat there hadn't been a litter of pups, either. *But why? Why would he lie?*

Mick looked at the farmer closely. "Are you absolutely sure there's no other reason you want to get rid of it, Alec?"

Mr. Tate sighed as if in deep regret. "As I said to you down at the Slaughtered Sheep, we're moving away. Goin' to Wookey Hole to live with our Linda. She won't take him *an'* our Gypsy."

"Truth now, Alec," pressed Mick. "How old is he really?"

"Eighteen month?" tried Mr. Tate.

"How old?" asked Mick again, this time leaning closer to the farmer.

"Three year," sighed Alec Tate. "And that's the truth."

"Has anyone else been interested in adopting him?" asked Jude.

"Nope," said Mr. Tate gloomily. "Only you."

"What will happen to him if you can't get anyone to take him?" asked Mick.

Narrowing his eyes, Mr. Tate solemnly raised a finger to his throat and slowly drew it across in a slicing motion.

"You mean . . . ?" said Jude, aghast.

"Yup," said Mr. Tate, nodding slowly.

All three looked down in horror at the dog, which appeared to be listening intently. Nat wanted to clamp his hands over the animal's ears, to spare it the dreadful knowledge.

"So, what you're saying is, if we don't take him, you'll have him put to sleep?" asked Mick.

"Summat like that," said Mr. Tate, turning purple.

Mick's expression hardened, and for a horrible moment Nat thought his grandfather was going to hit Mr. Tate.

"I'll not be held to ransom like this, Alec," he warned.

Tate shrugged. "Suit yourself, mate. Makes no odds to me either way. It'll be a long walk off a short pier for this ol' boy."

Nat risked a glance at the unfortunate subject of their conversation. The mutt had stopped its frantic blinking and stared directly at Nat. It was almost midday and the concrete yard offered no shade. Nat felt slightly faint, as though he were going to pass out. He shook his head to clear it, and noticed something peculiar about the dog's gaze. Its strange, amber-colored eyes had changed. Now they watched Nat, gleaming with warmth and intelligence. A golden glow shone from within, almost as though someone had lit a candle inside its head. Nat forgot the yard, the horrible farmer, his mum and granddad. He saw himself reflected, two tiny Nat Carvers, one in each eye, and inexplicably, he felt like smiling.

Then something incredible happened to Nat. *The sun went out.* Or, to be more accurate, for a few seconds, Nat was somewhere else. The relentless sun had been replaced by a glittering full moon. A cold breeze tugged at his clothes, freezing water lapped at his sneakers. Something lay at the shoreline, gently moving in and out to the rhythm of the shallow waves. Nat moved closer. He caught an unwanted glimpse of a big, pale dog, front legs tied to the back, fur sodden and matted. Its eyes were closed. It looked sad and lonely and *drowned*.

At once, Nat knew for sure that Tate would carry out his threat if they didn't agree to take the dog away. He felt the sun's rays again as the vision disappeared. The dog was still there, fixing Nat with its extraordinary golden eyes. Gradually they faded back to their usual color.

It made me see that, thought Nat. The knowledge left him panicky and cold inside, despite the heat of the day.

". . . or did you want to see the Labs at the stables?"

Nat shook his head, suddenly aware of the others.

"Sorry, what lavs, Granddad?"

"Labs," repeated Mick. "Would you like to see the Labrador pups up at the major's stables? I promised you a puppy, Nat. This . . . er, dog, isn't what I had in mind at all."

"Is he trained?" asked Jude.

"Oh, he's fine with sit and stay, the usual commands," said Mr. Tate airily.

The dog stood calmly next to Nat, its long legs wobbling slightly, its feet splayed out at gawky angles. It looked, thought Nat, slightly amused.

"Down," commanded Tate.

The dog yawned and walked off, its rear end swaying almost jauntily, as if to say, *"Stuff it, matey."*

"He don't know that one yet," blustered Mr. Tate, trying to regain some dignity.

Mick fiddled with his beard, lost in thought. Suddenly, he shot a contemptuous look at the farmer and grabbed Nat's arm.

"C'mon, Nat," he said. "I promised you a puppy. Let's go."

Tate and Nat looked alarmed, but for different reasons.

Nat turned to face Mr. Tate. "I don't have a choice, do I?" he said coldly. "If I don't take him, you'll kill him."

"I wuz only having a laugh," said Alec Tate uneasily. "My missus wouldn't let anything happen to that dog. Apple of her eye, he is."

Again, Nat knew instinctively that Mr. Tate wasn't telling the truth. Something very weird had just happened to him. Somehow, the dog had got into his head and shown him what might happen to it if Nat walked away and left it at the farm.

"Has he got a name?" he asked, rubbing the dog on its chest. In graceful slow motion, the dog rolled over onto its back and raised all four enormous paws in the air, inviting Nat to rub its belly instead. Another wave of happiness washed over him, the best he had felt since his dad left.

"He 'ent really got one," said Mr. Tate, "although the missus calls him Woody, on account of that's . . . er, I mean because he likes going for walks in the woods. What would you call him, young feller?"

Nat hesitated. When Mick had told him about the white German shepherd puppy, he had imagined it to be a small, cuddly creature, which, in time, would grow into a handsome dog. The creature in front of him was nothing like he had imagined. Its head looked a bit too large for its body and its legs looked almost too skinny to support it. The fur that wasn't covered in cow dung was patchy and thinning, as though someone had deliberately hacked at it with blunt scissors.

Nat shrugged. "White Fang?" he joked. He couldn't think of a single name to suit the scruffy creature.

"Storm?" suggested Jude.

"What d'you think, Granddad?" asked Nat.

"I think we ought to leave it," said Mick. "Go and see some more afore you make up your mind."

"I have made up my mind," said Nat. "I want this one, please. I want Woody."

"Well then," said Mick, "if you've made up your mind, it sounds as though you've settled on his name, too."

"Woody suits him." Nat grinned. "And he suits *me*, too."

"Not quite what me and your nan had in mind," said Mick, "but if you're sure . . ."

"Positive," said Nat firmly. "Thanks, Granddad."

To seal the deal, Mr. Tate spat into his hand and held it out to Mick. Nat grimaced as his granddad did the same. Then they shook on it; the deal was done. Mr. Tate bundled Woody into Mick's small car as though afraid he might change his mind. Somehow Nat managed to squash in beside him, trying not to choke on the smell of cow dung. The farmer slammed the door and waved them off, teeth flashing, skinny arms flailing like a windmill.

From the moment Mick turned on the ignition, it became clear that Woody was not a fan of car travel. His calm temperament disappeared in a display of such terrified behavior that Nat feared he was going to cause an accident as he thrashed in the confined space of the back-seat, his eyes flashing their strange golden colors and his nostrils flaring alarmingly. Nat and his family trundled off down the rough farm track to the main coast road, arms, legs, and furry bits entwined, as the boy tried in vain to persuade Woody to stay sitting.

Had they looked back, they would have been surprised to see the farmer still watching them, his shoulders slumped, the expression on his long face a mixture of misery and relief. They would have been even more surprised to see Mr. Tate do a very strange thing. He looked up at the clear blue sky and made the sign of the cross, his lips moving as if in prayer. Only when the car had disappeared did he make his weary way back to the yard. Although the sun was still hot, he shivered as he walked into the farmhouse.

"No going back now," he muttered under his breath.

CHAPTER 2

THE SLAUGHTERED SHEEP

By the time they had reached the end of the farm track, Woody's *Eau de Country Cow Pie* body odor problem had become so bad that Nat could almost taste it.

"Quick!" spluttered Mick, trying to breathe through his mouth. "Open the windows!"

Woody stuck his head out, his tongue snaking over the side of the window like a pink banner. Nat, by this time struggling for fresh air, stuck his head out of the other side as Woody's distressed moaning stretched into a soul-shriveling howl, so loud it made Nat's ears ring. At Temple Cross, Mick threw up his hands in surrender and made a decision he regretted exactly ninety-seven seconds later.

"I think a pit stop might be a good idea," he gasped; the smell was making him woozy.

As Mick pulled into the bustling market square, Woody was getting desperate. *"AAAAAAAWHHHHOO-*

OOOOOhhooooooooooo," he howled in anguish, his ears flattened against his skull. "WHHHOOOOOOOOOO HOOOOOOO OOOOH."

Jude's normally pale face was flushed brick red with heat and embarrassment as shoppers stopped dead in their tracks, craning their necks to see who or what was making such a racket.

"For goodness' sake, Nat, shut him up!" Jude yelled, putting her hands over her ears. "Everyone's looking!"

Mick turned off the ignition. Nat closed his eyes in a prayer of thanks as the howling stopped abruptly, and Woody poked his head between the front seats. Strings of saliva swung gently as he made little chuffing yips, blowing his furry cheeks out in distress. To a delicate traveler like Nat, no stranger to a sick bag himself, it wasn't hard to guess what was coming next.

"LOOK OUT!" he shouted. "HE'S GOING TO BE SICK!"

Across the square, the commotion had alerted customers eating their lunch outside the Slaughtered Sheep, a pretty sixteenth-century inn. Forks poised in disgusted dismay, they watched as the sweaty family spilled hastily out of the tiny car and Mick and Jude fled to the public toilets to clean up. Time seemed to stand still for a moment as the sight of Woody's last meal registered with the people outside the pub. Nat feared there would be a mass puke-a-thon, as everyone followed Woody's example and lost their overpriced grub in sympathy.

Fortunately, the response was less spectacular. A party of ladies who had been subjected to the clearest view of poor Woody cried out in disgust and promptly put down their forks, fanning their faces in distress. Everyone was staring; even the raucous laughter from the gaggle of older boys in the corner of the square had trailed off into a sort of horrified glee.

Oh, brilliant, thought Nat, *they're coming over.* Sensing trouble, he pulled on the piece of string that was Woody's leash and made an abrupt turn back to Mick's car.

His way was barred by a barrage of grinning youths. One of them, his hair so blond he'd looked bald from a distance, drew his lips back in a fake smile.

"That wasn't very nice, was it?" the blond kid asked in mock concern. He pushed his face threateningly close to

Nat's. His eyes were extraordinarily blank, the pupils tiny in the blue of the irises.

"Those are my dad's *paying* customers," he said. "How'd you like it if you were enjoying a nice bit of venison carpaccio and some dumb ol' dog spills its guts in front of you?"

The boy was at least three years older than Nat, and much bigger. Nat knew that whatever his answer was, it was never going to be the right one.

"I . . . I'm . . ." Nat's voice came out squeaky and scared. He tried again. The tone he was aiming for was confident and grown-up. "I'm *really, really* sorry about that," he finished.

As soon as the words were out of his mouth, he knew that he hadn't sounded sincere or confident. It sounded as though he were being sarcastic, and not in the least bit sorry.

"*Ooooh oooh,*" mimicked the boy in a high falsetto. "Hear that? He says he's *really, really* sorry! He don't sound very sorry to me!"

Vicious laughter rang out from the others, who had gathered around in a grubby corral of dirty necks and sneering faces.

Nat was just about to say something else when his arm began to vibrate with a remarkable noise. Low at first, it built to a rumbling, thunderous hum. It seemed to be traveling up from the piece of string to which Woody was attached. Puzzled, Nat looked down.

Woody's matted, dingy fur had puffed up to almost twice its size; his head seemed to be made solely of gleaming white teeth and blazing eyes. The rumbling grew to a bloodcurdling growl. The blond boy drew back sharply and brayed forced laughter.

"Has he got rabies or *what*?"

Badly shaken, Nat dragged Woody away from the gang.

"We shoots animals like that 'un!" shouted the blond boy. "Then we hangs 'em up by the legs for ten days, before we chops 'em up and feeds 'em to the pigs. You wanna keep it out of my way, or that's what'll happen to your dog!"

Spiteful laughter followed as Nat walked back to the car.

"Who was *he*?" asked Jude indignantly.

"Take no notice of him," said Mick. "That snotty little so-and-so is the landlord's son, Teddy Davis. He's a wrong 'un. I've had to have a few words with him in the past; that might be why he picked on you."

"Nat, are you OK?" asked Jude, concerned.

"Can we just *go*?" pleaded Nat. "Let's get him back into the car."

But Woody planted his lanky legs firmly into the dusty ground and refused to move any nearer to the car. Nat, the pukey smell still haunting his nostrils, wasn't sorry; if Woody wouldn't travel by car, then they would walk the rest of the way home. Still uncomfortably aware that Teddy Davis and his gang were sneering from their corner, Nat and Woody jogged past the inn out onto the main Temple Gurney road, keen to leave Temple Cross behind them.

Nat wondered if it would be all right to let Woody off the leash. He didn't fancy chasing after him in this heat if the dog got it into his head to leg it back to Temple Cross, but he decided to take a chance. He knelt down and untied the string from the battered old collar Tate had given them.

"Don't do a runner, will you?" he asked the dog anxiously, then instantly felt stupid. He'd have had a right shock if the dog had answered him! Nat thought again about the strange vision he'd had at Tate's farm. *Had Woody really been trying to show him what would happen if they didn't take him away?* He grinned to himself, feeling slightly embarrassed at even thinking such a thing. *As if!* Maybe he was coming down with heatstroke; anything else would be way too weird. Nevertheless, the image of the big, pale dog, hog-tied and drowned, had been enough to make up Nat's mind. He felt as though he really had saved Woody's life by taking him away from the horrible farmer.

And that was good, wasn't it? But something else nagged at Nat's brain. A saying, or an old proverb. Something like: "If you save a life, you become responsible for it." That bothered him a bit.

But as they walked through the leafy lanes toward Temple Gurney, he felt considerably cheered up. Woody had completely lost the depressed, downtrodden look he'd had at the farm. Free of the piece of string, he loped along, making weird little chuffing noises and occasionally turning around as if to check that Nat still followed.

Hot, tired, and grateful to reach home, Nat caught a glimpse of his grandmother smiling expectantly as she came down the path to greet them. By the time she had taken a proper look at the enormous creature, her smile had flattened into a grim line. Nat sensed she was not impressed.

"Look at the size of it!" she shrieked. "I thought Alec Tate said it was a puppy."

"Ar," said Mick, hurrying out of the shed at the sound of his wife's voice. "He *was* a puppy, about three year ago."

Nat's grandmother, who was called Apple on account of being round and rosy, was very wise, and had wobbly arms and a fearful temper. She tutted impatiently at the sight of the enormous animal and swatted her husband away like an irritating insect when he tried to hug her.

"Trust you to buy a dog the size of a pony," she scolded. "I should have known better than to let you do a deal with that man Tate."

As Nat and his mum hid their grins behind their hands, Apple eyed Woody with deep suspicion. She asked Nat to hold him still while she walked around the dog's vast bulk. "Funny-looking," she murmured to herself.

She turned to Mick. "Doesn't look much like a German shepherd to me. Did you ask to see its parents?"

"Should I have?" asked Mick, knowing he should have.

Apple shook her head in disbelief. Her small, chubby hands delved into Woody's smelly coat while he sat patiently. She inspected his enormous teeth and examined his ears. Her final verdict was no surprise.

"I have *never* smelled anything as bad as this creature in my *entire* life," she declared, fanning her face with a plump hand. "Give him a bath, Nat; he's not coming anywhere near my kitchen like that. And what's going on with his fur? It looks as if it's been cut with a knife and fork!"

Apple watched as Woody eagerly followed his new master into the garden. The expression on her face suggested she was trying very hard to add up a difficult sum, or remember something important, but couldn't quite put her finger on what it was.

Leaving Woody to inspect the garden, Nat climbed the stairs to his attic bedroom. Despite the unwanted upheaval from London, he was happy with his room at the top of his grandparents' house. When he looked out of the windows, which were slanted and fixed into the roof, he could see the woods, and if he strained his neck really hard to the left, he could see the sea. Mick had put up shelves for his books, and there was a smell of fresh paint and new wood.

Nat loved books and the different worlds you could escape to through reading. When he had started school, he just didn't seem to have that much in common with any of the other kids he met. He knew it bothered his mum a good deal more than it bothered him, so he was careful to make sure she never found out he didn't really have any friends. Like most mums and dads, his parents could be a source of much embarrassment; but while other mums didn't appear that concerned about global warming, recycling, or rescuing the whales, his own seemed determined to save the world single-handedly. Last winter, he had been dragged along with her on a demonstration to protest against cell phone towers and, unfortunately for Nat, the scenes of both him and his mum being forcibly removed by two burly policemen had been on TV. Nat's usual strategy of keeping a low profile had been blown, and he held Jude completely responsible for the abuse he got from the other kids at school.

And on top of the unwelcome media attention, someone had spread a rumor that his dad had been sent to prison.

As is so often the case, though, the truth of the matter was more complicated.

Nat's dad, Evan Carver, was an inventor, or rather, an inventor of useless and often dangerous contraptions. His last brainwave, *HovvaDogga*, a hovercraft designed to help disabled dogs, had seemed flawless in blueprint. Sadly, the prototype had resulted in near-fatal injuries for its doggy pioneers, a dachshund and a Pomeranian, which had both been too fat to walk, but evidently not too fat to be propelled fifty feet into the air when the hovercraft sped up in hot weather.

Another disaster, *Action Pants!*, a robotically enhanced trouser press, had attacked an elderly man, imprisoning him in his closet for three hours. The old man had accused Evan of assault and battery, for which he had been arrested then released on bail.

With the trial pending, Evan Carver had tried to get a legitimate job, but without success. And since money was scarce, he resorted to borrowing from a shady moneylender to make ends meet. When it became clear he couldn't pay back the money he owed, he was visited by a couple of large, well-built gentlemen who had threatened to snap off his arms and legs. Not surprisingly, Evan panicked and jumped bail. He hastily arranged for Jude and Nat to leave London and stay indefinitely with Jude's parents in Temple Gurney, a small town in the southwest of England. The last Nat had seen of his dad was a tiny stick figure waving from the stern of a ferry bound for Calais, France.

Nat remembered how he had sat in sulky silence as Jude urged their ancient camper van through the parched countryside. He had looked up from his book in alarm when she'd pulled off the road on the edge of a dense wood. There was a lot of purply-black smoke pouring out of the engine.

"Stay inside," Jude had said bluntly, dragging open the rusty door on the driver's side. As she struggled to get the cap off the radiator to put some more water in, Nat couldn't help feeling a blinding flash of anger at his dad for getting them into this mess and leaving them to cope on their own. He watched glumly as two enormous black crows unraveled the pink innards from an unidentifiable squashed animal.

When Jude returned, she breathed a sigh of relief and popped the lock down on the door, motioning to Nat to do the same.

"Nearly there now," she said breathlessly. She turned to look at him, her forehead creased with worry. "I want you to promise me one thing, Nat."

Nat dragged his gaze away from the carrion crows.

"I want you to promise me that you won't go into these woods alone, *ever*."

He had rolled his eyes at her. "Funny you should mention that," he said sarcastically. "I was just about to wander off on my own into those horrible-looking woods, because that's the sort of thing I do for fun."

"Don't give me any lip," snapped Jude uncharacteristically. "It's just . . . well, I suppose it's because I was always frightened of them as a child. People have a habit of going missing in them."

Nat glanced nervously at the woods. Did the trees look closer together than when they had arrived? Surely not, but there *was* something spooky about them: impenetrable and threatening. Nat shivered, wishing they were any-where but here.

When their old camper van had eventually trundled into the village, there was a sign to welcome them:

TEMPLE GURNEY

WELCOME TO OUR TOWN.

PLEASE HONOR OUR WILDLIFE.

As far as Nat could see from the amount of roadkill littered about the place, this request hadn't been taken too seriously by the car-driving Temple Gurnians. Someone had scrawled underneath in black marker, *Twinned with the Moon.*

Now, back in his room, Nat's thoughts returned to his dad. Although it is very wrong to listen at doors (you rarely hear anything good about yourself), he couldn't help over-hearing his grandparents in conversation a couple of days ago. He'd hovered outside the kitchen, checking regularly over his shoulder in case his mum caught him.

"And I worry about that poor little soul," he'd heard Apple say.

"Which one?" asked Mick, his voice muffled by the piece of bread and butter he had scavenged.

"Nat. He's too sensitive."

"Oh, he'll be all right," said Mick. "Bit imaginative, that's all. Remember Gary?"

Both his grandparents chuckled, making Nat cringe. Gary had always been there for him when he was small. Trouble was, Gary had been an imaginary friend. And he had been a unicorn.

"And I worry about Jude, too," said Apple. "She's making herself ill over That Man."

Nat pursed his lips in annoyance. Lately, Apple always referred to Dad as "That Man."

"Ar, well, that's a different matter," said Mick, his voice taking on a sterner tone. "Do we know when he'll be back to face the music?"

Nat heard a *plop* as Apple's ample rear hit a chair.

"I'm not sure he will be," she answered quietly. "He's joined his father's circus."

"Oh?" said Mick. "He's a bit old to run away and join the bloomin' circus, isn't he?"

"John Carver's Twilight Circus of Illusion," said Apple scornfully.

"Eh?" Mick was a man of few words when eating.

"I mean, really!" said Apple. "I don't expect much from Evan, but I would have thought John was old enough to know better. The two of them are daft enough to think they're going to make their fortune!"

Nat sneaked back into the living room; he'd heard enough. His father's plans for fortune-making didn't interest him anymore.

Still, later that same evening, Nat had been overjoyed (but played it very cool) when at last his dad called. He didn't mention what he had overheard, in case it got him into trouble. Instead he told his dad about Mick's plan to get him a dog as a special welcome present.

"A dog?" Evan had exclaimed. "Brilliant idea. Get a proper one, though, not one of those small yappy types, like those high-flying dachshunds or Pomerwhatsits!"

Now, in his bedroom, Nat couldn't help smiling as he remembered their conversation. He missed his dad like crazy, and knew he was an accidental criminal, a *victim of circumstance*, his mum had explained earnestly. He wondered what his dad would say when he saw Woody. Since leaving the horrible Farmer Tate, Woody seemed less like an untidy, smelly mutt. In fact, Nat thought proudly, his new pet looked very much like a *wolf*.

CHAPTER 3

CAMELLIA LANE

Temple Gurney, like the rest of England and Wales that summer, sizzled with record-breaking temperatures. It was so hot that Apple swore she could feel the tiny hairs on her arms crisping in the heat, and could rarely be coaxed out of the shade.

A few days into Nat's strict grooming regime, Woody almost squeaked with cleanliness and smelled of something Apple called "Hallo Vera." Nat was surprised to find that, minus the caked cow dung, Woody's coat had turned out to be pure white, although uneven patches of pink skin still showed through. He agreed with Apple: It *did* look like someone had hacked at Woody's coat with a knife and fork, but Nat couldn't for the life of him think why anyone would do such a thing. Weirdly, it seemed that whoever had given Woody his hacked-off hairdo had allowed the fur to grow freely on the top of his head and neck in a kind of halfhearted Mohawk. And Nat was glad to see that when Woody's coat was dry, it shone like spun silver.

"What a *beeyoodiful* example of canine coiffure!" Nat grinned, proud of his efforts. He stepped back to admire Woody, who yawned, making the supersonic jet noise again.

"Sorry if you're bored," he apologized. He supposed Woody couldn't care less whether he smelled. Nat checked that no one was around, then looked deliberately into Woody's amber eyes.

"*Are* you bored?" he whispered.

Woody gazed back unblinkingly.

"Come on, Woody," said Nat, feeling slightly foolish. "Are you receiving me?"

Woody stared back — his eyes were still the usual mild amber, not the flashing golden colors Nat was hoping for. Woody yawned again and scratched his belly, punctuating every scratch with a satisfied grunting noise. Nat grinned. When Woody scratched the side of his face, he looked so dumb that the idea of him possessing supernatural powers was suddenly very funny. Nat got the giggles. Whenever he tried to stop, he started again until his sides hurt and he felt weak. He plopped down on the grass next to Woody, who had stopped mid-scratch, big ears cocked, looking goofy and confused.

"Sorry," Nat apologized. "I wasn't laughing at you, I swear! It's just that . . ."

Nat glanced again at Woody, who was looking at him now as if he had gone completely bonkers. "It's just that"—he lowered his voice—"I thought you'd called to me with your mind, and that maybe you made me see what was going to happen to you if we didn't take you away. I guess I must have imagined it after all."

Woody placed a large paw on Nat's shoulder; maybe he was reminding him he hadn't finished grooming him just yet. Nat picked up the brush, thinking hard. He was still convinced that Mr. Tate had lied about Woody and his reasons for getting rid of him.

An idea had begun to form in his overactive imagination. Nat had compared Woody to one picture of a German shepherd dog and another of a wolf. The wolf looked more like Woody, except that Woody had much longer legs and his weird Mohawk hairdo seemed to suggest some sort of mane. His paws were enormous! They were almost twice as big as Nat's own hand and the toes were long: unusually long, and joined together by a thin webbing of skin.

"Like a *wolf*," he told his mum when she and Apple came to see how he was getting on with Woody's beautification.

"Did you know that only wolves and Newfoundland dogs have webbed feet?" he asked her excitedly.

"Or Woody may have just been born lucky!" Jude laughed. "Just because he has a bit of skin joining his toes doesn't mean we have a wolf among us."

But to Nat, this was just another check mark in the box for his big THEORY about his new pet.

"OK then, Mum," he said patiently. "Have you asked yourself why Woody never barks?"

Jude shrugged. "Maybe he's got a sore throat from all that howling we had to put up with the other day."

"Exactly!" cried Nat triumphantly. "Howling! He howls but he never barks. And look at him. Tell me he doesn't look just like a wolf."

Jude sighed. "Yes, he does, but so do most German shepherds, that's why they frighten people."

"And why did Mr. Tate seem so keen to get rid of him?" Nat was warming to his subject. "I bet it's because Woody is one of those illegal imports, you know, a hybrid wolf, a cross between a wolf and a dog."

"Nat, listen to yourself," said Jude mildly. "What on earth would somebody like Mr. Tate be doing with an illegally imported dog?"

"Money?" said Nat, knowing he was losing ground.

"D'you know how much granddad paid for him?" asked his mum gently.

"No," admitted Nat, a little sulkily.

"The promise of a barrel of Apple's organic cider."

"Yes, but . . . ," protested Nat.

"Nat, you're almost thirteen years old," sighed Jude. "It's time to rein in your imagination a bit."

Nat narrowed his eyes. He was *never* going to live down Gary the Imaginary Unicorn! He was just about to give his mother four other reasons why Woody could be an illegal import when Apple interrupted them.

"What on earth . . . ?" Apple exclaimed. She had been helping to brush Woody's Mohawk and was now peering at something intently.

There was a strange collection of livid blue marks on Woody's skin.

"Looks like a tattoo!" marveled Nat, straining his neck to get closer. "P'raps Mr. Tate got it done to brand him, in case Woody got stolen."

Apple frowned and shook her head. "From what I know of Alec Tate, I don't think he's the sort of man to spend money on a dog he wanted to drop off the end of the pier. Anyway, don't dogs get tagged electronically for that type of thing nowadays?"

"Is it a word, or a design?" Nat asked, peering into Woody's fur again.

"I can't see it properly, he's too hairy!" said Apple, laughing.

Nat held Woody's head while Apple tried to part the fur again, to get a better look.

"I think it's a word," she said. "Look, it's letters in a circle. There's an *R*, and an *O, T, E, U, S,* and the last one, a *P*."

"*ROTEUSP?*" said Nat, puzzled. "I'll get a pen."

Between them, they wrote down the letters, and Apple decided the circle began with a *P,* making the tattooed word *PROTEUS.*

Curious, Jude joined in.

"Proteus was the name of a Greek god who could change his shape," she said. "But why on earth would someone want to tattoo it on a dog?"

"No idea," replied Nat. "We'll have to ask Mr. Tate; he's bound to know."

Apple stared at the tattoo, her plump face serious. She pursed her lips and followed Jude back into the house, muttering something under her breath that Nat couldn't hear.

The incident with the tattoo wasn't the only thing that Nat needed to think about. Staying with his grandparents was always interesting, and living with them was even more exciting. Apart from her organic cider and cheese-making (which made Apple famous from Temple Gurney to Temple Meads), she had an uncanny gift for nursing sick wild animals and birds back to health. In the winter, her shed became home to orphaned hedgehogs too weak to hibernate. In the spring she would expertly fix the broken wings of tiny fledglings with cardboard and masking tape. Nat was particularly interested in helping Apple set the birds free.

Before "Clearing for Takeoff," as she always called it, she would fill an eyedropper with a clear liquid from one of the assortment of bottles she kept locked in the cupboard. The nozzle of the eyedropper would be gently inserted into the bird's beak, and it would guzzle greedily at the offered treat.

"What *is* that stuff, Nan?" Nat had asked her on more than one occasion, as he helped her remove the splint from a healed wing.

"Jet fuel," she said, concentrating, "it'll keep him out of trouble, give him a little boost."

Nat was positive it *wasn't* jet fuel; that would be poisonous for sure. But whatever it was, it made the birds' feathers shine with health; their eyes were bright and inquisitive; and they looked *bigger* somehow.

Nat was also curious about the abundant garden at 11 Camellia Lane. The heat wave had resulted in a local ban on watering, and yet his grandparents' grass was a lush, almost neon green. The neighboring lawns on Camellia Lane were brown and shriveled like tobacco. Surely his grandparents weren't flouting the restrictions?

When Nat questioned Mick on the greenness of their lawns, Mick just winked, tapped the side of his nose, and said, "Ask me no questions, and I won't tell you no lies."

It hadn't been the most helpful answer.

Nat dragged his thoughts back to the present. He gave Woody a final brush and went off in search of his grandfather.

The orchard appeared deserted except for Mick's increasingly unreliable and eccentric lawnmower, but there was no sign of its owner. Then Nat saw him coming out of the shed with a small bottle full of bright green liquid. He was stripped to the waist, apart from his suspenders and a red neckerchief to stop his neck from burning, his eight earrings dancing in the sun. He seemed oblivious to Nat's presence.

Nat watched as Mick sprinkled a few drops on the beautiful green lawn. The liquid behaved in an extraordinary way: It hovered above the ground and dipped and jived for a few moments before being absorbed into separate blades of grass, which appeared to fold over the liquid and soak up any trace.

"What's that, Granddad?" Nat shouted, making Mick jump about three feet in the air.

"Good Gawd above, lad, I didn't know you were there!" Mick spluttered. "You shouldn't sneak up on people like that!"

Nat was hurt. "Sorry. I just wondered what it was. It makes our grass a lot nicer than everyone else's."

"Ar," agreed Mick, shoving the cork back into the bottle. "That information is only available on a strictly need-to-know basis," he said, and tapped the side of his nose again. Then he made Nat mow the lawn, as he said his heart rate had been shaken off course by Nat making him jump like that. By the time Nat had finished and cleaned the lawn-mower well enough to satisfy Mick's high standards, the sun was disappearing into the horizon, and Nat was dying for a cold drink.

A peachy glow flooded the back garden. The adults sat outside enjoying a glass or two of Apple's organic cider.

"There you go, boy," beamed Mick, handing him a small amount in a teacup. "That'll put hairs on your chest."

Nat put his lips to the rim, trying not to gasp as the fumes hit his senses, his eyes watering, his nostrils contracting with the smell. He took a minuscule sip.

"Mmmm," he said politely, feeling the liquid blaze painfully down his gullet. Suddenly he clawed at his throat and fell onto the grass, groaning and twitching. Apple and Jude watched in alarm.

"Aaaargh," moaned Nat, "the hairs are growing *inside* my chest, I'm *dying, aaaargh!*"

Woody rushed to Nat's side, pawing at him, making anxious little yipping noises.

"Oh, stop, Nat!" cried Jude. "Poor Woody thinks you're really in trouble."

Mick roared with laughter; Apple flicked a dish towel around his ear, making his earrings jangle.

"That dog's going to make a brilliant companion for you, Nat," said Mick thoughtfully, when they had finished their supper. "He's loyal to you already. Let's see how many words he knows."

Calling Woody to his side, Nat made him sit, stay, and fetch, and Woody obeyed every time.

"Look at that," said Jude admiringly. "It's almost uncanny. It's like he understands every word you say."

Nat didn't notice his grandmother's odd expression as she watched Woody perform his tasks faultlessly.

It was getting late. Jude rose from her rickety deck chair, declaring that she was tired and going to bed. Nat glanced at his mum with fresh concern. He watched as she walked down the path to the house, her white shirt gradually disappearing into the growing darkness. He drew comfort from the fact that his mum and dad spoke nearly every day on the phone—surely that meant they weren't getting a divorce or anything? Nat was worried; what would happen if Dad was serious about this circus? Would that mean Nat and his mum would have to move again? Even go abroad? Would his dad be like a fugitive? Would Woody be able to go with them? *One thing's for certain*, thought Nat to himself. *They can think again if they're planning on leaving Woody behind!*

Apple and Mick got up shortly afterward. It was time to indulge in their favorite Saturday night pastime: Tonight they were going to watch *The Outlaw Josey Wales*, their second favorite movie—the first being *The Good, the Bad and the Ugly*—starring their ultimate screen god, Clint Eastwood. Nat went up to bed. He had seen *The Outlaw* eleven times already.

Before the movie started, in the privacy of the comfy living room, Apple turned to her husband.

"That Alec Tate took you for the fool you are, Mick Smith," she said, looking stern. "That creature was no more born on his farm than you or I."

Mick bowed his head in shame.

"Reckon you're right," he agreed miserably. "That tattoo on his neck proves it, I guess. But if Woody's from *up there*, why is Alec Tate involved?"

"I don't know," said Apple, worried. "And I don't need to remind you what happened the last time livestock escaped from Helleborine Halt!"

Mick shivered. "But you don't think that Woody is . . . ?"

"You better hope not," said Apple softly, "because if he is, we're all in trouble."

CHAPTER 4
HEAVY GLOW

Despite his tiredness, Nat lay awake. The windows in the roof were both open, but because his room was at the top of the house it was still baking hot. Apart from the occasional gunfire sound effects wafting up from the movie two floors down and the whir of the fan, the night was still and quiet. As his eyes closed, he thought fleetingly about the tattoo on Woody's neck, but no sooner had the thought surfaced than he fell asleep.

When he woke, Nat felt even more uncomfortable, but cooler; a refreshing breeze was blowing his hair back from his sweaty forehead. He opened his eyes groggily. The book-lined walls of his bedroom had gone, replaced with trees, their foliage glowing eerily in the moonlight. He was lying on a bed of pine needles and leaves; no wonder he was uncomfortable. *Where am I? This is a dream, right?* But if it *was* a dream, he had never experienced one so real before. He looked up at the enormous moon, shielding his eyes — it was so unnaturally bright.

Disoriented and frightened, Nat rose from the woodland floor and brushed his pajama pants with trembling hands. *Maybe I've been sleepwalking,* he thought in alarm. *It all seems so real.* He felt a stab of terror. It *was* real: Somehow he'd found himself in the forbidden East Wood in the middle of the night, *and he was not alone.*

Out of the corner of his eye, he saw a rustling in an enormous fan of bracken that framed the moonlit path. He watched, unable to move, as a long, thin figure unfolded itself from the middle of the foliage like a charmed snake emerging from its basket. At first, Nat thought it was a man, but as his eyes adjusted to the moonlight, he saw that whatever it was, *it was not human.* The skin was a mottled, dead gray; the thin legs bowed but topped with powerful thighs, roped with muscle. The hideous torso, sprinkled with coarse black fur, was attached to the head of a wolf with fangs that grew snaggled and pointed. The eyes were a wicked, raddled orange, burning malevolently as they fixed on Nat, making him feel shaky and weak. He tried to move, but his legs wouldn't do what he wanted them to, which was to run for his life. A scream rose in his throat but died in his mouth, and he realized with sickening horror that the wolf thing was getting closer, although it hadn't appeared to move. It leered just a few feet away from him, and Nat seemed to be drifting toward the creature against his will; he had a surreal sensation of being gently lifted off the leafy floor of the woods and floating . . . floating, close enough to the wolf thing to look deep into its eyes. Nat felt himself relax as he stared into their fiery depths, and wondered why he had been afraid.

It's only a nightmare, he thought to himself dreamily. *Any second now I'll wake up . . . Uuuuughh!* Barely inches away, the savage, corrupt stink of the wolf thing suddenly tore into Nat's senses like smelling salts. Gagging, Nat snapped his head back, the hypnotic effect broken, his eyes watering. The wolf thing made as if to grab him with an enormous misshapen paw, and as Nat turned to run, he fell forward, hitting the floor with a bone-jarring *thump*, and woke up, surrounded by familiar things again.

He laughed shakily. He was right. Nothing but a stupid nightmare, and now he had fallen out of bed. His heart was banging in his chest like a chorus of bongo drums, and his pajama top was sopping wet with sweat. He had an urge to call out for his dad, but reality hit him. His dad was gone, and there was no way he would call for his mum and upset her.

He closed his eyes and breathed in — *hmmm* — and breathed out — *hoooo* — the way his mum had taught him to relax. The bedroom was aglow with a cold white light; a light so strong, it felt *heavy*. Nat groaned. On top of the hideous nightmare, the streetlights outside were working overtime. *Hold on, though. We're in the country; there are no streetlights outside.* And even if there were, they weren't tall enough to shine into his room; the slanted windows in the roof were too high. Still badly shaken, Nat got up off the floor, his legs feeling weak and bendy like rubber, and stood on tiptoe to look out of the window.

A vast full moon hung in the velvety-blue night sky. The enormous white orb threw its penetrating light so strongly that the darkened areas on its surface — the seas, the plains, and the craters that were usually invisible — glowed like silver.

Memories of the horrible creature and how it had stunk of dark, wet places surfaced, and Nat shuddered, feeling jumpy and itchy and strange. Knowing sleep would be impossible, he crept out onto the landing and past his grandparents' room, smiling slightly at the appalling noise of both of them snoring. It sounded just like several pigs snorting down slop. Apple always denied snoring, but she was even noisier than Mick. Nat wondered how they could sleep with that racket going on, then he remembered how loud the TV gunfire had sounded. They both must have been going deaf.

He opened the kitchen door and went in to get a drink of water. As he reached up into the cupboard for a glass, a noise made him freeze. Despite the heat, cold shivers slid up and down his limbs, and the tiny hairs at the back of his neck prickled and fizzed. He strained his ears to catch the noise again. It was as though someone was crying softly; someone who was upset, but didn't want anyone else to hear.

"Mum," he hissed, "is that you?"

No answer. Nat hesitated; if it was his mum, maybe she wouldn't like it if he barged in on her. He wondered if he should just go back to bed. But the weeping continued, and Nat forgot about the glass of water.

He crept down the corridor to the scullery, opening the door onto the light of the moon. It lit up the garden so brilliantly that Nat could see as well as if it were daylight.

The crying sounds stopped abruptly. There was a movement in the corner by the washing machine.

"Woody?" croaked Nat. The spit he needed to talk with had almost dried up. "Come on, boy."

There was a shuffling noise, like cloth being dragged, but what came out of the shadows was nothing like a dog. Nat's mouth dried up completely.

Wrapped within Woody's red, striped blanket was a boy. A boy of about Nat's own age. They stared at each other.

"Wh . . . wh . . . who are you?" stammered Nat. "And where's my dog?"

The boy shook his head, sniffling. Nat noticed that underneath the blanket the boy appeared to be naked. His eyes went as wide as they could without popping out of his head.

"I . . . look, excuse me, but where's Woody, and . . . hey! Why are you naked?"

As soon as Nat had spoken, something clicked in his brain. He looked hard at the stranger, noticing how his cheeks were stained from crying. There was something odd about his eyes. They were an unusual light golden brown. In the dark shadows, they appeared to glow.

Noooo, thought Nat, confused. *It can't be . . . can it?*

"Are . . . are you who I think you are?" he stammered.

The boy just stared, his eyes glimmering golden light.

A purely selfish thought popped into Nat's head. Just when he thought he had a dog, this happened!

At last the boy spoke, in a halting, gravelly voice that sounded as though it wasn't used very often.

"You can . . . call me Woody," he said quietly. "But I'm not . . . a *dog*."

Nat's legs gave way, and he slid to the floor. All this was too much. This was Gary the Unicorn territory. Whoa. He wasn't ready for this! The boy sat down, too, wiping his eyes on the corner of the striped blanket.

Suddenly, Nat slapped himself, hard, across the face: *THWACK!* The boy jumped at the sound and looked at Nat in alarm.

"Why did you . . . do that?" he asked, his curiosity stopping his tears.

"Because I'm dreaming," said Nat, shaking his head. "That's it. I must be! The moonlight's turned me mental! I'm really still in bed, and you are still a dog, so good night to you." He got up to leave.

Suddenly, the strange boy grabbed hold of Nat's pajama sleeve. *"I'm not a dog,"* he repeated.

Nat swallowed, trying not to let the boy see how scared he was. He glanced at the boy's hand, sensing enormous power and strength. *And his fingernails!* To Nat, they looked alarmingly like claws.

"Well, what are you, then?" asked Nat bravely.

"Wolven," the boy stated, removing his hand. "Shape-shifter."

Nat stared in horror, remembering his dream.

"A *werewolf*," he breathed, shrinking away from the strange boy and getting ready to run. He wondered if he could make it before the boy turned into a wolf and ripped out his heart, or whatever it was that werewolves did. As though he could read Nat's mind, the stranger sat down again, and put his shaggy head in his hands in despair.

Nat hesitated. There was something about this strange person that was so familiar, so *Woody-like*, that he wanted to believe he would be safe. He cleared his throat to show he was still there. The boy raised his head and looked at Nat with sad eyes.

"OK," said Nat, almost to himself. "Werewolves turn into wolves at the full moon, or they do in the books I've read. I've never heard of a wolf turning into a boy."

The boy shook his head again. "Not werewoof, *Wolven*."

Despite his fear, curiosity was getting the better of Nat. "So do you, um . . . change back again in the morning? Sort of like a werewolf in reverse?"

The boy shivered and nodded. "Can't stop it . . . Dunno when it'll happen. Al . . . Alec Tate didn't like it."

Nat thought of the dreadful Tate. "You mean he *knew*? He knew you weren't really a dog?"

The boy nodded. He lowered his voice. "It's not so . . . complic . . . comp . . . it's *easier* if I stay Wolven. But I needed . . . to warn you . . ."

Nat's eyes narrowed as he remembered something. "*Hey.* I've rubbed your belly!"

The boy smiled for the first time. It was a sweet, familiar smile, but Nat couldn't help noticing the way his sharp, white teeth caught the light of the moon.

"I'm still Woody," said the boy gently. "Still your friend. Please help."

Nat tried to think straight; he felt an instinctive liking for this strange boy, who obviously needed help, but then he remembered the horrific wolf thing in his nightmare. He shook his head, confused and petrified. *What if this boy turned into that . . . creature?*

Again as if he could read Nat's thoughts, the boy's smile faded, his expression heartbreakingly sad.

"Wolven are not monsters," he said simply. "Woody was *born* this way, not *made*, like werewoofs."

"Were*wolves*," corrected Nat, remembering the hideous wolf thing in his nightmare.

The boy stood up and wrapped the blanket tightly around his thin body. Nat watched, mute, as he hesitated at the door leading to the moonlit garden. Then, suddenly, the boy disappeared into the night. Nat was left sitting on the floor, wondering what on earth to do next. But as he was about to find out, when the astonishing happens, you just get on with it.

CHAPTER 5

AN UNWELCOME VISITOR

For three generations, the Tate family had worked the farm and neighboring lands at Temple St. William. But the prizewinning dairy herd of doe-eyed Jersey cattle had long gone. All that remained of the family farm, apart from the land and buildings, were a few elderly sheep and some eggless chickens.

Alec Tate cut a lonely figure as he watched the last of the sheep being loaded into his neighbor's trailer. On completion of the sale, loads of money would be paid into Alec's account by some fancy London developers. He was surprised and disappointed to find that the thought brought him no joy at all. He gazed across the land that would not be owned by a Tate much longer, and wondered briefly if his father and grandfather were turning over in their graves.

After a moment he turned away. Much of the pasture-land bordered the vast East Wood, which to Alec represented two hundred horrific acres, and the sight of it unfailingly made his belly churn with greasy unease.

In the 1960s, when Alec had been a relatively young man, parts of the wood had been cordoned off in order to study the biodiversity of the area, and designated "Sites of Special Scientific Interest." East Wood was notorious for people going missing within its boundaries, but it also had something special to offer, especially for folk who liked to study such things. Controversially, the woods were owned and managed not by the local Temple Gurney Wildlife Trust, which would be usual in the circumstances, but by the government.

A few months after the government takeover, following the discreet arrival of researchers and scientists, wild rumors began to fly around Temple Gurney and neighboring villages. Locals began making their own assumptions about what went on up at Helleborine Halt, which was the name of the elegant country mansion now used as the research headquarters. The general consensus of local opinion was that the government was studying species rather more diverse than a few rare flowers.

Stories of hairy, orange-eyed beasties lurking in farm outbuildings were never proved, but the fact remained that people disappeared without a trace from time to time, and sheep and cattle were slaughtered in the fields, often savagely mauled beyond recognition. The government was forced to issue a statement to the tune of "We Have Nothing to Hide," and Helleborine Halt, a few miles from Alec's farm, was opened to the public to prove their point.

Alec remembered that he and his late father had enjoyed the same tour as everyone else. There had been nothing much to see, apart from a few mutts in cages smoking thirty cigarettes a day to test whether smoking really *was* bad for humans, and some sad-looking baboons in full makeup, who were not wearing it just to look their best for visitors. In those days, this appalling exploitation of animals had been legal and, regrettably, the good people of the region were satisfied.

Alec shook his head, dragging his thoughts back from the past, and waved halfheartedly at his neighbor, now trundling off down the dusty track in his battered old Jeep, pulling the trailer full of sheep behind him. If Alec had realized that, deep down, he did possess a conscience, he would have understood that the uneasy roiling in his guts was guilt, not indigestion, and no matter how much he drank to dull his senses, it showed no sign of going away.

That's that, then, he thought to himself, feeling as old and dried-up as an empty corn husk. Sighing deeply, he swung his leg awkwardly over the five-bar gate, wincing at the *click* of his artificial hip.

Alec's melancholy was rudely interrupted by a volley of barks, startling him, making him lose his balance and topple off the gate into an untidy heap. He looked up in astonishment as Gypsy, his elderly Welsh collie, stood before him, the hackles rippling and bristling at the back of her neck.

He struggled to his feet. "What the . . . ?" he began irritably. He squinted in the direction of the farmhouse to see what had upset her. There were no strange cars as far as he could see, but Gypsy shot off toward the courtyard in a black-and-white blur, her body low to the floor, ears flattened against her skull. Alec Tate had a bad feeling about this, but then, like most people who are unlucky enough to be born pessimists, he had bad feelings about most things.

Instinctively, he pushed himself close to the side of the house, trying to keep up with the collie as she crawled her way, commando-like, across the front garden. If someone had rung the bell, Ophelia, his wife, wouldn't have heard it from the attic, where she was packing away three decades' worth of junk.

Alec reached the front of the house, starting to feel a bit daft. There was no one there. Now Gypsy had drawn herself up to full height and was looking quizzically at the front door.

"You must be getting old timers' disease," he chuckled to Gypsy. The old dog lay down on the porch with a slightly embarrassed expression on her graying muzzle.

On the porch, Alec Tate set about removing his gum boots. This involved hopping around on one leg, falling over a lot, and muttering swear words. In fifty-odd years of Wellington-boot-wearing, he had never mastered their removal without this ritual. Panting, he walked through the hallway into the back kitchen and put on first his fuzzy slippers, and then the kettle. He couldn't be bothered to shout for Ophelia, although he was surprised she wasn't making the tea. *Probably still sulking*, he thought. She hadn't spoken to him much since she'd found out what he had done with Woody.

He was still suffering palpitations from his earlier fright, so he began the comforting ritual of tea-making. He put a used tea bag into a mug and fished around in the saucepan cupboard where he'd recently discovered that Ophelia hid the ginger snaps. He poured the boiling water into his mug and pressed the tea bag into the side of the cup with a spoon, carefully removing it for another time. Then he went into the parlor with a plate of the delicious treats (most of the box—he was very greedy, and partial to their sharp taste) and stopped dead in his slippered tracks.

Sitting in Alec's favorite chair was the dim outline of a man. He was obviously a much taller person than Alec Tate, because his legs were drawn up awkwardly, almost reaching his chin. On closer inspection, Alec noticed he was dressed in a sharp suit, the knife-edge creases of his pants enhancing the odd shape of his legs.

Alec's first reaction was one of outrage. This fellow's crisp suit reeked of "government agency." He had seen enough government officials to last a lifetime since the foot-and-mouth epidemic, which had spelled the end for his farm. That and the ban on hunting. He'd had month after month of finding his chickens headless — not *eaten,* mind, just killed for fun by a rogue fox that would've been finished off by the local hunt in the good old days. It was no wonder that Ophelia often said Alec's deep suspicion of all things governmental had turned *him* mental.

But something told Alec that this visit was not about foot-and-mouth disease. Nothing would have made up for watching his livestock burn on pyres visible from as far away as the Welsh Mountains anyway.

The figure leaned forward, as if in greeting, and Alec recoiled slightly at the gleam of malice shining from the man's eyes. The first fingers of fear stroked Alec's heart. He decided to brazen it out, which was, although he didn't know it yet, probably the bravest thing he had ever done in his life. It was a shame Ophelia wasn't there to witness it. Come to think of it, where was she?

"If you're from DEFRA, you've got a bloomin' cheek!" he roared, red-faced. "And who invited you to sit in my chair?"

The man got up slowly, aided by a gold-topped, old-fashioned cane. Alec watched in fascination as his legs lengthened beneath his body.

"Your dear wife admitted me," said the man pleasantly. His accent was posher than the Queen's, and he had a curious way of speaking; it sounded strangely muffled, as though the mouth were the wrong shape to make words properly. "Unfortunately, the dear lady feels unwell."

Alec groaned inwardly. This bloke wasn't from DEFRA. He had a good idea where he might be from, though.

"If you've hurt her . . . ," spluttered Alec.

"I assure you, she is not hurt. Well, not much," the man replied, in his quiet, conspiratorial manner. "But I digress! It is *you* I have come to see. Allow me to introduce myself."

He held out his right hand. Alec stared at it in undisguised horror. This chap appeared to have some sort of unfortunate excess hair problem. The proffered hand was more like a paw, covered in thick black hair, the blackened nails twisted into sharp, cruel-looking points.

"My name is Lucas Scale. I am not from DEFRA — the Department of Environment, Food, and Rural Affairs. I am," he announced rather grandly, "a representative for the Ministry of Defense. Here is my card." He held out a piece of plastic.

Alec stared at the man, ignoring the card.

"From up at Helleborine Halt?" he gulped.

Scale ignored him. "I have some questions I require you to answer."

Alec feigned ignorance. "I thought that place was no longer any business of the government's."

"I'm afraid you have been misinformed," said Scale smoothly. "I won't, as you charming countrymen say, beat around the bush, so: WHAT HAVE YOU DONE WITH HIM?"

As the words blasted from Scale's mouth, Alec Tate's scant hair blew back from his forehead in a rush of putrid air.

"Wh . . . ? I don't know what you're talking about, mate," said the farmer, who, despite his fear, didn't appreciate being shouted at in his own living room.

"Oh, I think you do, old man," whispered Scale. "To refresh your memory, I believe he had the rather quaint name of Woody."

"That ol' *dog*, you mean," said Alec, forcing a wavery smile. "I shot it. Worried my new sheep, see."

Alec didn't see it coming. Scale's pawlike hand grabbed him roughly around the back of his neck.

"I'll worry *you* in a minute," said Scale. "So I'll ask another question. Who paid you to look after my Wolven?"

"I dunno what you're talking about," squeaked Alec, now thoroughly scared.

Scale released his hold, sending Alec spinning across the room, knocking over the television, which he hadn't finished paying for yet.

"Take me to the body, then," snarled Scale. "Where's it buried?"

Anger buoyed Alec's fright. "I burned it," he snarled back. "Like you lot made me burn my cows, when there weren't anything wrong with them. Foot-and-mouth, my ar —"

Alec stopped in midsentence. To his horror, Scale's face had begun to change. The nose and mouth began to push outward to accommodate large canine teeth, which lengthened and pointed downward in cruel spikes. Coarse black hair sprouted from Scale's hairline and merged with the wolflike pelt that spilled over his collar. And his eyes! Alec watched in dreadful fascination as they started to glow with a dirty orange light. The blackened nails lengthened into vicious claws, which shone dully in the light of the setting sun. Scale flexed the claws with intent, as if he were going to pluck out one of Alec's eyes. Mercifully, at this moment, Alec's brain decided to call a halt to the proceedings, and he slid gracefully to the floor in a dead faint.

CHAPTER 6
A FREAK AND A WEIRDO

As he raced out of the house and through the garden gate, Nat half hoped there would be no sign of the boy formerly known as his dog. But when he reached the top of the lane, Nat was surprised to feel relieved when he saw the stranger, still wrapped in the striped blanket. The boy stood motionless, appearing to sniff the night air, as if he were making a decision about which way to go. Panting and dripping with sweat and nervous excitement, Nat ran to catch up with him.

"Wait!" he gasped. The boy stood patiently as Nat tried to catch his breath. "S . . . sorry. I'd just had a terrible nightmare about some kind of werewolf thing," stammered Nat, "and, well . . . I realize you're nothing like the creature in my nightmare. I'm pretty sure I can trust you."

"You . . . helped me," said the boy, in his curious, halting manner. "I'd never hurt you — or your people."

"Mr. Tate was going to *drown* you!" cried Nat, remembering the vision of Woody, his front legs tied to his back, at the water's edge.

"He was desperate," said the boy sadly. "Sc . . . scared, too."

Nat's eyes lit up. "So you *did* show me with your mind. That was telepathy, right?"

"Telly . . . tele*vision*?" said the boy, his face suddenly brightening.

"No, not tele*vision,*" said Nat, "tele*pathy*. It's communicating with your mind." Nat felt out of his depth. He didn't know if the boy understood what he was trying to say. "Can you do it again?"

The boy shrugged. "Sometimes yes, sometimes no."

"Like earlier?" Nat remembered. "When I tried to do telepathy in the garden?"

The strange boy nodded. Nat began to feel more confident. There were so many things he wanted to ask.

"But why was Mr. Tate so desperate to get rid of you? Was it because he thought you were dangerous? Like a werewolf?"

Woody shook his shaggy head. "Tates were . . . *hiding* me," he explained. "I'm being hunted."

"But why? Who . . . ?" asked Nat, eyes wide.

"Very Bad People," said the boy darkly.

Nat looked impressed. "Should I still call you Woody?" he asked.

The boy shrugged. "Don't care . . . just want to stay."

Smuggling Woody up the two flights of stairs to Nat's bedroom was not as easy as Nat thought it would be. The loud honking sounds from Mick and Apple's room made Woody clutch Nat's arm in fright.

"What's that?" he whispered, his eyes gleaming gold.

"My grandparents." Nat grinned.

Woody exploded into a fit of strange noises. Nat looked at him in alarm, then realized Woody was laughing. He hastily ushered Woody up the remaining stairs, frightened to death that they'd wake everyone up. The full impact of what had happened hit him like an express train. *This is crazy*, he thought. *Is it really happening, or am I truly losing it?*

In the loft bedroom, Woody was overcome with curiosity. Nat had given him a pair of shorts to replace his striped blanket, and now Woody was bounding around the room like an excited puppy.

"*Telly!*" he exclaimed, and shot over to the old TV Nat had brought with him from London. "Yours?"

Nat grinned. "It's nothing special; we don't have satellite or anything fancy."

Woody busied himself sniffing in all the corners and under Nat's bed. He was ecstatic at Nat's collection of *Star Wars* figures, picking each one up and sniffing it carefully. Nat watched, bemused, noticing that Woody could easily pass for a human, except when his eyes flashed the brilliant gold colors that seemed to mean he was excited or upset. Privately, Nat thought that Woody's weirdly chopped, pale blond hair needed immediate attention, and the unibrow wasn't a good look, either.

"How old are you?" he asked Woody curiously.

"Same as you," replied Woody, who was still busy exploring.

Nat felt his world wobble again. *Oh, no, that couldn't be right!* If Woody had been a pup when he arrived at the Tates', it didn't make sense. He was sure Mr. Tate had told them that Woody was three years old.

"You *look* about the same age as me," said Nat doubtfully. "That would make you almost thirteen. But that can't be right!"

Woody stopped and thought for a minute. "'S'right," he assured Nat. "Wolven reach adult ess . . . essence in first three years. One year Wolven is the same as four years human."

Nat smiled weakly. "Wolven reach *adolescence* in their first three years?"

"Sure do," Woody replied with an American twang. "'Phelia Tate said so."

Oh, wow! thought Nat. *This is getting wilder and wilder.*

"So how d'you learn stuff?" asked Nat curiously. "Did you go to school or have a private tutor or . . . ?"

Woody looked surprised. "Telly and telepathy. Better than school."

Nat remembered something. "D'you know anything about Proteus?" he asked.

Woody looked up from a model Chewbacca. "Whateus?"

Nat reached his hand up to Woody's neck, pushing aside his hair. "Didn't you know you have a tattoo on the back of your neck?"

Woody craned his neck to see the livid blue letters in the mirror.

"Apple found it," remembered Woody. "Why?"

"I don't know," said Nat grimly. "But it could have something to do with whoever is hunting you. I could ask my granddad what he . . ."

"*No!*" shouted Woody, eyes flashing. "Thought I could . . . trust you!"

"You can, of course you can!" cried Nat. "I just thought . . ."

"The more people know, the worse it'll be," said Woody desperately. "Old Mick wouldn't believe you anyway."

Nat agreed with Woody on that point. He thought it would be highly unlikely anyone would believe him ever again. He would be a laughingstock if he told them what had just happened to his dog.

"We could threaten Tate with the police, make him tell us who's after you, or where you'll be safe." Even as the words came out of his mouth, Nat knew this wouldn't work, either.

"'Phelia and Alec have . . . have gone," Woody stammered. "Something . . . *someone* . . . is coming for them. I can feel it."

"Could you try doing that vision thing again?" asked

Nat, hoping to calm Woody down. "Show me stuff, like you did at the farm?"

"I'll . . . try," said Woody haltingly. "What . . . do you want me to show you?" He was so eager to please, it made Nat feel humble.

"I just wondered if we could communicate like that more when you're a . . . when you're in animal form," said Nat. "It would make life a lot easier."

Woody looked crestfallen. "Too hard," he said glumly, "unless you're telepathic, too. I can only show pic . . . pictures, not words. Used to do it with 'Phelia Tate sometimes; helped show her where to find stuff. Takes a long time . . . very tiring." He seemed to remember something. "I could do it easily with Gypsy, though."

"Who's Gypsy?" asked Nat, puzzled.

"Sheepdog," said Woody.

"Mr. Tate's sheepdog is *telepathic*?" asked Nat, amazed.

"Lots of animals are," explained Woody patiently. "Humans, too, till they kind of lost . . . er . . . lost . . ."

"Lost the knack?" interrupted Nat.

Woody nodded. "Dogs can be a bit . . ."

"Thick?" broke in Nat.

Woody grinned. "B . . . boring. Cats are better. Gypsy just talks about sheeps."

"Sheep," corrected Nat.

"Sheeps," insisted Woody.

"I s'pose you could do the two-way thing with another Wolven, though," said Nat excitedly.

Woody shook his head sadly. "Dunno any."

Nat felt awkward. "Sorry," he said. "What about your parents?" As soon as he had asked the question, he could have kicked himself.

There was an awkward silence as Woody's bottom lip wobbled.

"I . . . think they're . . . dead," he said sadly. "Th . . . think that's why I'm being hunted."

Although there was nothing worth watching, Nat turned on the television very quietly to cheer Woody up. It was like magic: Woody sat cross-legged in front of it, hypnotized, repeating the catchphrases on the quiz shows and humming tunelessly along to the commercials.

When Nat woke hours later, he felt disoriented and confused, as though he had been on a long-distance flight to a far-off land where everyone had gone completely nuts.

He sat up abruptly, memories of last night flooding his brain with a sick dread. Woody! Where was he? He had visions of Woody wandering into the kitchen, still dressed in his shorts, and Apple and Mick openmouthed at the sight of a strange boy helping himself to the food in their fridge.

Nat threw on some clothes and leaped down the stairs three at a time, cannoning into the kitchen where, just as he'd feared, his grandparents sat, openmouthed.

"Where's the fire?" asked Mick mildly as Nat shot by, frantically scanning the garden for his new best friend.

"Where's Woody?" Nat asked breathlessly.

"In the downstairs toilet," replied Apple, pouring his tea.

"What's he doing in there?" asked Nat, confused.

"Drinking out of it." Mick grinned. "I always put the lid down, but he's a clever beggar, he pushes it up with his head."

Nat plopped down in his chair, relieved. Over a break-fast of three fried eggs, crispy bacon, black pudding, and beans, he relived the events of the night before in his mind.

He was convinced it had really happened and it hadn't all been a weird dream. And anyway, where on earth would he have got the idea about a Wolven from? His knowledge of werewolves was limited to movies and comic books and, as Woody had tried to explain, he certainly wasn't in the same league as the vicious killers portrayed in horror films. Look how wimpily he had reacted to his gran and granddad's snoring! Nat grinned in delight at the memory. No, Woody definitely wasn't dangerous. But then Nat remembered how he had reacted with that blond boy, Teddy Davis, the landlord's son from the Slaughtered Sheep. He had looked terrifying. Nat grinned again.

"What's so funny?" asked Mick. "C'mon, share the joke."

"I was just thinking what a lovely day it is to go to the library," said Nat offhandedly.

"Why d'you want to be shut up in a stuffy library on a day like today?" asked Apple. "I thought you and Woody were going out in the boat."

"I need to look up a few Internet sites about werew . . . dogs," explained Nat. "You know, health and behavior and stuff."

"Well, you'll have to leave Woody outside when you go in," said Apple, arms wobbling hypnotically as she scoured the frying pan. "They only allow guide dogs in there."

Nat had ventured into the town a few times since their arrival in Temple Gurney, and although he could appreciate it was very old and undeniably pretty, he had not been very impressed by it. On Fridays the market square was transformed by the traveling farmers' market, but like many rural towns and villages, there wasn't much to do in Temple Gurney apart from outdoor stuff. Nat had spent most of his time at the beach with Jude, and Granddad had taken them out in his boat, the *Diamond Lil*, a few times.

The library was a prefabricated building at the end of Main Street, flanked by some large trees, which at least promised shade for Woody.

"I'll just get whatever information I can on werewolves and Wolven, so we can figure out what to do next," Nat told Woody, tying his leash to one of the smaller trees. An old man walked by and smiled at Nat, tickled by his assumption that the boy was explaining his book-borrowing plans to his dog.

Inside, the library took on surprisingly large proportions and was blessedly cool after the heat of the pavement. Nat was also surprised to see an impressive rank of computers, almost as many as he had been used to at the library at home in London. He approached the librarian, a cheerful-looking man dressed in brown cords and a shirt and tie topped with a short-sleeved pullover. Nat explained he was new in Temple Gurney and would like to join the library. Coins were exchanged for an hour's use of the Internet.

He typed "Wolven" into the search engine. Disappointingly, nothing related to a species called Wolven came up, only people and places. He replaced it with "Werewolf." He wasn't surprised when it informed him he was at page 1 of 630,000 results. He tried being more specific and typed "Reverse" in front of "Werewolf." It took forever to load, and he was sure it would come up with nothing.

Then up it popped: Score! Nat scanned the page.

http://www.lycan-therio.net/random/werewolf.htm

A Reversal in Lycanthropy — A Study into
the Essence of Werewolves and Theriomorphs by
Dr. Susan Berryman — University of Chicago

Nat started to read, but it was written in a very dry, academic style, and didn't once mention Wolven. He caught the eye of the librarian.

"Would it be OK if I printed this for my summer project, please?" he asked.

The librarian peered over his shoulder. "What have we here? Ah . . . ten pages about lycanthropes?"

Nat felt his cheeks redden. "Er, no. Werewolves, actually."

"Lycanthropes, theriomorphs, shape-shifters, whatever term you prefer." The man nodded. "The werewolf is the best known example of lycanthropic behavior, but there are plenty of other forms."

While Nat waited for the pages to be printed, something caught his eye on the desk.

Dog Show! Nat thought. Maybe there'd be prize money. He could do with some extra cash now that he had a Wolven as a pet. And anyway, it might be fun to enter Woody, especially if there were obedience categories. If Woody behaved himself, there was a chance they could win! As he picked up the flyer, a sudden breeze appeared to come from nowhere, and a richly embossed card fluttered across the desk. Nat's eyes widened in surprise.

"Can I have this to take away please?" he asked the librarian. The librarian peered at the card Nat held in his hand. He looked puzzled.

"That's funny," he said, almost to himself. "I'm sure that wasn't there just now, but yes, of course. Sounds as though it will come in very handy for your project."

Nat read the card again.

> ## LYCANTHROPES IN THE TWENTY-FIRST CENTURY
>
> ### A TALK BY IONA DE GOURNEY, AUTHOR AND ENCHANTRESS
>
> MEADE LODGE, EAST VALLEY
> TEMPLE GURNEY
> TEL 905-676-0129
>
> SATURDAY, AUGUST 3RD @ 8:30 P.M.
> REFRESHMENTS PROVIDED

Thanking the librarian, Nat took both the flyer and the card to show Woody, and opened the door.

Nat reeled. It was like walking into an oven. He felt the same otherworldly lightness of being he had sensed at Tate's farm. Then he realized. It wasn't just the heat;

something was very wrong, and Woody was trying to warn him! Sweat poured down Nat's face as he tried to steady himself. But as quickly as it had arrived, the feeling passed. Wiping the sweat from his eyes, his stomach flipped in panic when he saw a crowd of teenage boys circling Woody. At the heart of the throng was a familiar blond figure. He groaned: He was toast.

For a panic-stricken moment, Nat debated whether to leave Woody outside the library and come back later. He knew Woody could take care of himself. Then, realizing that if he didn't face his tormentors now, he never would, he took a deep breath and approached them, trying to walk without his knees knocking. Teddy nudged his nearest companion and hooted ugly laughter.

"Aw look, it's the new girl," he guffawed. "You stalking me, *Natalie*?"

The other boys laughed and Nat flushed, surprised that Davis even knew his name.

"My name is *Nat*, not Natalie," he said. The words came out a little higher than usual—even to Nat, his voice sounded like a girl's.

"Is that like *Gnat* with a silent *G*?" Teddy asked mock-innocently. "Are you a gnat?"

The gang screamed with laughter, making annoying gnat sounds.

"No," said Nat, finding his voice, "not *G-N-A-T*, Nat." He glanced anxiously at Woody, who was watching intently.

"Not Gnat?" Teddy grinned, shaking his head. More hysterical laughter.

"No, *not* Gnat. Nat," said Nat, annoyed with himself for falling into Teddy's stupid word game.

"Well, Nat," said Teddy, grinning hatefully, "you're certainly as insignificant as a gnat, but I think Natalie sounds so much prettier, don't you?"

One of the other boys piped up. "Yo, Natalie, let's have a borrow of your cell."

"I don't have a cell," said Nat, knowing what was coming next.

"Then let's have a look at your watch."

Nat was dismayed. The watch had been a birthday present from Gramps Carver. It was an expensive one, and was backlit by a cool blue light. It said in the instructions that it would still work even if you dived to two hundred meters. Nat hadn't had the chance to try that out yet.

"What are you waiting for, *Natalie*?" jeered a pimple-faced boy with a dirty Megadeth T-shirt stretched over his pudgy stomach. "Take it off and give it to Tiger."

Nat realized Pudgy was talking about Teddy Davis; Tiger must be his nickname. He felt the inexplicable need to burst into hysterical guffaws. Tiger! What a joke. He clenched his fists so that his nails cut into the palms of his hands. *Oh, no, don't laugh, please don't laugh.*

He took a deep breath. "Get lost, *Tiger.*"

A strong sense of déjà vu washed over him, almost like the vision he'd had before. But this time, he recognized that the menace in the low rumbling coming from Woody's throat was for real, his lips lifting away from his teeth — which appeared much longer and sharper than usual — and his eyes flashing gold.

"Or what?" said Teddy coldly, his eyes narrowing. "That dog lays a whisker on me, *Natalie*, and I'll make sure it's put to sleep quicker than you can say Rip Van Winkle."

Nat knew he would carry out his threat. "Woody, no!"

he commanded, taking a firmer grip on Woody's collar. "Down, boy! Heel!"

Teddy pressed his pale face up to Nat's.

"I don't like your face and I don't like this stupid-looking excuse for a dog," he hissed. "That ugly mutt's a freak an' you're a right weirdo. Just give me the watch, an' we'll call it quits."

Nat opened his mouth to protest, but knew it would do no good. He undid the watch in silence and handed it to the blond bully. Teddy looked surprised for an instant, but snatched the proffered watch. Then he shoved Nat hard. He fell over and crashed painfully to the ground, ripping his elbow badly on the curb. Woody pulled hard, his hackles up, trying to get at Davis, but Nat kept a tight hold on his collar, despite the pain. Davis looked down at him with contempt.

"Now get out of here."

Wincing, Nat inspected his damaged elbow; the blood was running freely down his arm in rivulets and splashing onto the ground. He put his arm around Woody's thick neck and used it as a lever to pull himself up. The gang watched him silently; their earlier high-spirited spitefulness had turned to cold menace.

Badly shaken, Nat struggled to pull Woody back toward the safety of Camellia Lane. Growling ferociously, with his teeth still bared, the Wolven still looked like he wanted to cause serious damage to the gang. When Teddy Davis was out of sight, Nat stopped to get his breath back.

"You tried to warn me they were there, didn't you?"

Woody stopped growling and made a chuffing noise, wagging his tail halfheartedly.

"Well, next time do me a favor, don't bother with the telepathy." Nat grinned a little shakily. "Just howl your head off!"

CHAPTER 7
WHO'S THE MUMMY?

Ophelia Tate padded noiselessly along the landing like a great panther, her heavy body automatically programmed to move silently under threat of enemy invasion. She had served in the medical corps during Britain's Falkland Islands conflict and seen plenty of active service, so she knew she would still be handy in combat. She had been unlucky this time, that was all. An egg-shaped lump where Scale had struck her head with his walking stick throbbed dully in her left temple.

Ophelia twitched with unspent rage. She was livid at being taken unawares; hadn't she known that sooner or later they would receive a visit? She had just stepped out of the shower and put on her bathrobe when he'd struck, taking her by surprise. Although she had never met Scale face-to-face before, she had heard of his love of violence, and wasn't surprised that he had come to do the interrogation himself.

As she came to from the crack on the head, she thought she heard Alec shouting. He would never win a prize for best husband, but despite the fact he had sold Woody behind her back, Ophelia couldn't let him suffer at the hands of the creature in the parlor.

Creeping down the staircase, she hardly dared breathe. Her ample bosom heaved majestically within the quilted polyester bathrobe, her nylon-clad feet lightly skimming the synthetic carpet, working up an electrical charge that could have powered half of Temple Gurney. She was so charged with rage and static electricity that her long blue-black hair escaped from its braids and frizzed out in a wiry Medusa-style hairdo. She reached the bottom step and hesitated, her head cocked to one side as she listened.

Lucas Scale jerked his misshapen head toward the living room door, as if he sensed something outside. He had reversed his change for now, but his strange orange eyes and snaggleteeth still looked unmistakably evil.

Alec Tate slowly came to from his faint, and seeing Scale move, he felt a twinge of hope that someone might come and rescue him from this madman. Alec tried to remember what had happened before he'd passed out, but his mind blocked out the memory. Was Ophelia all right? What if Scale had hurt her badly . . . or even . . . ? Scale looked capable of anything.

Still pretending to be unconscious, Alec peered surreptitiously at his tall, bowlegged interrogator. Scale's nostrils flared in and out, his body tense. At last, satisfied there was no one coming and realizing that Alec was back from his swooning fit, Lucas Scale resumed his interrogation, punctuating each question with a painful shake to Alec's throat.

"Did you really think I would believe you'd killed my Wolven, cretin?" he snarled, inches from Alec's face.

"Oi, oi . . . who are you calling a cretin?" spluttered Alec Tate, trying to recover some dignity. "I swear, he worried my sheep, he was a lunatic."

Scale shook his head in mock sadness. "If you do not tell me, I will simply maim you for now, then send worse interrogators. They will rip the truth from your lying lips, and tear your lily liver from your body."

Tate closed his eyes. He could not imagine a worse interrogation than the one he was on the receiving end of right now.

Out in the passageway, Ophelia's fury reached two hundred degrees Fahrenheit. Over her dead body was she going to let Scale, who had been responsible for her cousin Robert's downfall, terrify Alec into telling him where Woody was. She bit her lip. Alec had done a very bad thing by letting Mick Smith and his grandson drive off with such a valuable secret. If Scale found out where Woody had gone, Mick and his family would be in terrible danger. . . . *Oh, good grief, what had Alec done?*

There was silence now; all she could hear was the old clock ticking in the hallway. The sun had crept below the horizon, and the evening air felt thick and clammy.

Sneaking a look through the crack in the doorway, she was able to see her husband, suspended several inches above the floor. He looked like a weasel being hypnotized by a snake. Ophelia dared not wait any longer. If she did, she knew that her husband would shortly be missing an eyeball.

"AHAAAAAAAAAYYA!!" she screamed as she shot across the floor like a fiery comet, propelled by an energy even she was shocked to have mustered. Scale didn't have time to compute what had hit him. By now, the amount of static electricity manufactured beneath Ophelia's bathrobe was making a humming noise like a top and sending out sparks. Tate watched his wife in pure wonder, sparks flying from her body as she clashed with the fireplace's metal guard screen. Scale was knocked into the hearth, losing his cane, his long, bowed legs scrabbling as they tried in vain to get a grip on the polished tiles. The next thing he was aware of was a huge bottom encased in sapphire blue polyester bearing down on him.

"Gedoff!" he screamed.

Ophelia was enjoying herself. She pressed down with all her weight. Scale had never known such painful humiliation.

"Who's the mummy?" asked Ophelia grimly.

Scale was silent, trying hard not to breathe, let alone talk, through this terrible ordeal.

"Who's the *mummy*?" Ophelia asked again, pushing down even harder.

"Yooouuu! Yoou are!" screamed Scale. "I beg you, madam, gedoff me!"

Ophelia motioned to Tate to get the rifle they kept hidden in the cocktail cabinet.

"If I get off," she panted, "you'll leave this farm and never come back?"

"Yeesss!" Scale yelled. "Whatever you say!"

Ophelia got up slowly, her huge bottom receding like an eclipse of the moon. Scale took a while to get up from the tiles without his cane. Alec noticed with satisfaction that the feet jammed into Scale's shoes were more like hideous paws: No wonder he needed a cane to walk.

Eyeing Alec Tate, who had by now retrieved his rifle and was pointing it at him, Scale staggered out of the sitting room. The Tates watched in silence as he scuttled down the drive, looking over his shoulder as if to make sure that Ophelia wasn't following him.

"Told you someone would come here looking for Woody, didn't I?" said Alec Tate, his squashed face more glum than ever. "He'll be back, too."

Ophelia stayed silent, but had to admit to herself that maybe Alec had done something right after all. It was just as well Woody was no longer on the farm; Scale's flaring nostrils would have smelled him out, that was for sure.

"Then we leave for Wookey Hole tonight," she said, tossing back her Medusa hair dramatically. "We'll leave this forsaken place forever."

CHAPTER 8
THE AMAZING, MANGY MUTT

Like many people who have the misfortune to find themselves being bullied, Nat didn't feel the need to share the incident outside the library with his mum. He was pretty sure he could avoid Teddy "The Tiger" Davis for the remainder of the summer. Compared with the rest of his problems, it didn't seem that important.

The information he'd found out at the library had been about as useful as a mesh umbrella, and he didn't feel they had made progress with the quest for Woody's origins. Despondently, he picked up the flyer about the annual Temple Gurney Country Show and Fair, and had been pleasantly surprised to find that it would be quite an occasion, with real rides like bumper cars and a Tilt-A-Whirl, and bands playing in the afternoon and evening. But it was the part about the classes in the dog show that caught Nat's eye:

DOG WITH THE MOST APPEALING FACE

BEST-BEHAVED DOG

BEST-DRESSED

OBSTACLE RACE

DOG WITH THE BUSHIEST TAIL

"I bet that's four out of five we'll win," said Nat, sharing his thoughts with Woody in the shade of the weeping fig tree. Seeing the hurt look on Woody's face, Nat laughed. "OK! OK! We can enter the Appealing Face contest, but don't make your eyes go all weird."

Satisfied, Woody made his favorite supersonic jet noise as he stretched out in the late evening sun.

The hot weather had been constant throughout the summer, and the day of the Temple Gurney Show was no exception. Apple and Jude had changed into cotton summer dresses to try to stay cool in the heat, and Mick put on his favorite Hawaiian shirt, which was pink and orange and clashed horribly with his skinny red jeans. Woody had been unable to resist rolling in the carcass of a putrid seagull, which meant another dip in Hallo Vera. This time, the smell was so bad that Jude had dabbed sweet-smelling patchouli oil behind his ears.

"He looks really handsome, thanks to your efforts," said Jude, stepping back to appreciate Woody's debonair new appearance. "Look at his face. It's like he knows we're talking about him."

If only you knew, thought Nat, smiling.

The show field was packed. There were long white tents full of flowers and vegetables arranged on trestle tables that seemed to stretch on forever. Apple had entered her "mums," which Nat found out was short for *chrysanthemums*, and Mick had entered his onions, which were roughly the size of small planets. The show ring, where currently the fire brigade was demonstrating putting out fires, was where Nat and Woody would compete later on. There was a smaller tent, too, outside of which numerous men whom Nat recognized as Mick's pals from the

94

Slaughtered Sheep stood gossiping and drinking bacony-smelling cider from plastic cups as big as pitchers. Nat was amazed to see the crowds that thronged to the fair: He hadn't realized there were so many people living in Temple Gurney.

Nat looked to see if Mr. Tate was standing with the other farmers outside the cider tent and was disappointed to see there was no sign of him. He would have liked to ask him some questions about Woody, starting with the mysterious tattoo.

Mick fought his way out of the crowd, clutching melting Popsicles for all of them. Apple and Jude went to browse inside the "Blue Moon New Age" tent, and Mick spotted a few of his cribbage friends outside the cider tent. He was licking his lips expectantly.

"Be all right on your own for a bit?" he asked Nat.

Nat nodded. "Don't forget to come and watch the dog show, though."

"Wouldn't miss it for the world." Mick grinned. Then his face turned serious. "But listen, Nat. Don't speak to any strange people. I mean it, mind."

Nat gave a wry smile. Most of the people in Temple Gurney were strange because he hadn't been introduced to them, and, the rest were . . . well, just *strange*.

With Woody on a loose leash, the pair wandered through the crowds, drawn to the carnival rides. It was exciting with the rattle and hum of the fairground people, and the delicious smells of popcorn and cotton candy made his mouth water. Little kids lined up to have their faces painted with weird and wonderful animals. One four-year-old, his face painted as a dog, growled menacingly at Woody as they went by. Woody growled back, baring his enormous wolf teeth. The kid dropped his ice cream and ran screaming to find his mother. Woody drooled at the sight of the melting ice cream and pounced. When it was gone, he looked guiltily at Nat, who was doubled over with laughter.

Nat was enjoying himself until, after a few minutes, he noticed that Woody had started to behave oddly. He was standing very still, showing his teeth in a silent snarl, saliva dripping from his mouth.

Nat froze. There, sitting by the enormous public address speakers, with a couple of his least attractive friends, was Teddy "The Tiger" Davis.

At first, Nat was horrified, then he relaxed slightly. Davis was spouting off about something or other, his dumb buddies hanging on to every word he said. Nat was pretty sure Davis hadn't seen them.

Woody's lip curled again, his eyes flashing.

"*Don't* make your eyes go all weird again," hissed Nat. "Let's just try to keep a low profile."

He spotted his family settling down on the grass to watch the dog show and wandered over. The dog handlers from the Temple Cross police department were displaying their talents. Everyone attending the show seemed to be watching, including Davis and his friends. Nat could only hope that they wouldn't stay for the next event, but they showed no sign of moving from their spot on the opposite side of the ring.

Apple was excited. "Good luck, Nat, show 'em what you're made of!"

Mick clapped Nat on the back as they followed the other entrants through to the waiting area. There appeared to be two judges for the "Dog with the Most Appealing Face" competition.

Nat and Woody were in the junior class. Their fellow contestants were a blond girl with a very handsome

Doberman, squabbling twins who were showing a Shih Tzu and kept wrestling its leash from each other, and a beautiful golden cocker spaniel accompanied by an earnest-looking boy with matching golden hair and a squint.

Nat knew they were outclassed; entering had been a massive mistake. Woody was doing his best, but in his eagerness to please, he was trying too hard. He sat awkwardly, bolt upright, with a goofy grin on his face. Nat noticed he had pink goo on his whiskers from the cotton candy, and brown goo on his chest from the stolen ice cream. They were the first to be inspected by the judges. A skinny lady with a wilting flower arrangement in her hair and more lipstick on her teeth than on her lips spoke kindly to Nat, as if sorry for him.

"And what is your . . . ah . . . beautiful dog called?" she asked.

Nat told her.

"And what breed is Woody?" she asked politely.

"He's a German shepherd mix," replied Nat.

The other judge, sweating in a tweed suit, snickered. "What's he crossed *with*?" he asked. "A Wookiee?"

"He's a lovely doggy," said the lady, glowering at the tweedy man. "Good luck, dear."

Nat smiled back weakly, hoping Woody wouldn't take offense. The judges moved down the line to the pretty spaniel.

Mick and Apple were giving him thumbs-up signs, and Jude was smiling encouragingly. Nat bristled with embarrassment. It looked as though the judges were coming to a decision. The tweedy man was just about to step up to the microphone to announce the winners in reverse order when a commotion occurred at the ringside.

"Oi, Natalie! Look lads, it's *Natalie* and her Amazing Mangy Mutt!"

There were titters from the crowd.

"Dog with the Most Appealing Face?" Teddy yelled. "Most Gimpy Expression is more like it!" A few others in the crowd laughed. Nat's face was bright red and he could feel sweat trickling down the back of his shirt.

Woody stood up and strained against his leash. "Just ignore him," said Nat, holding on tightly but sensing big trouble ahead.

"Ah, listen! Baby Natalie's talking to her ickle doggy like he's a real person," chortled Davis, enjoying the attention of the crowd.

In a moment of dreamlike slow motion, Woody charged. Pandemonium followed. Nat, his hand nearly wrenched off, let go of the leash and watched in horror as a snarling Woody hurtled across the ring to where Teddy Davis was standing. The smile slid from Teddy's face as he turned around and pushed his way through the crowds, who were thoroughly enjoying this unexpected entertainment.

Nat soon lost sight of Woody and, followed by Mick, he fled across the ring trying to catch a glimpse of him. Bystanders scattered, tables were knocked over, vegetables and homemade cakes went flying, people were screaming.

Mick was soon out of breath, but Nat ran on without him. A few exhibitors tried to stop Nat and show him the damage his dog had done, but Nat had one thing on his mind. He couldn't bear to think of the consequences of Woody biting Teddy Davis. Nat searched around the back of trucks and trade stands, but he found nothing.

It was only when he was trudging back, dodging the people whose stands had been wrecked, that he suddenly sensed Woody was near. Following his instinct, he ran through a pathway made out of parked cars, but what he saw there made him cry out in panic.

Teddy Davis was lying on his back. Standing over him, pinning him to the dusty grass, was Woody, legs splayed out, hackles stiff. His eyes were glowing and drops of his hot saliva dotted Teddy's T-shirt.

"Get it off me," pleaded Teddy, hot tears running down his face. "Get it away from me."

Nat rushed over and dragged Woody away by the collar. Teddy got up slowly and awkwardly. Nat, still suffering from shock, went to help him.

"Get lost!" shouted Teddy. "Tell anyone about this, and you'll be sorry you were born."

Nat stood silently, not knowing what to do.

"That dog's a lunatic," said Teddy, trying to stifle another sob. "I'm gonna tell my dad about him, and the police will make you have him put down."

Nat and Woody watched him as he hobbled back toward the crowds.

"Nice one, Woody," said Nat wearily. "I thought you said that Wolven were a peace-loving ra . . . ?"

The words died on his lips and he shook his head in disbelief.

"Oh, no, not now! Please no!" He felt as though all the air had been sucked out of his lungs. From within the fur at both sides of Woody's head poked two unmistakably human ears.

CHAPTER 9
CRESCENT

Woody's back arched like a cat's and a wild keening noise came from his open mouth. His front and back legs shot out from underneath him, forcing him to lie flat in the dust, his head whipping from side to side. To Nat, it looked as though he was being pulled apart by something or someone unseen. The thick white fur on his face became thinner, then disappeared completely, as if blown away by a sudden wind.

Nat was horrified—he felt powerless to help. Woody's muzzle shrank, his neck lengthened, and soon the top half of him was boy-shaped. Then nothing. The rest of him, the lower half, stayed resolutely Wolven. He writhed helplessly in the dust, his wolf legs unable to support him.

Nat had no option but to drag Woody along, trying to find a safe place to hide him. *If someone comes along . . .* Nat shoved the thought out of his head.

As Nat dragged him behind a VW van painted with huge purple and green swirls, Woody was still moaning, as if in terrible agony.

"What's the matter?" asked Nat, still in shock. "Why can't you complete the change?"

"Dunno," gasped Woody. *"Stuuuuck!"*

Nat didn't know how much more he could take. Dealing with Woody in two separate identities was one thing, but half boy, half Wolven? *What if he stayed like that?* If only his dad were here. The thought of his dad was the last straw, and Nat had to bite his lower lip to fight back the tears.

Whether it was a reaction to seeing his friend so upset or whether it would have happened anyway, Nat didn't know, but Woody's change got going again. The fur on his lower half disappeared, and his legs straightened out. Last of all, his paws narrowed into human feet. The transformation was complete. A bewildered, naked boy crouched in front of Nat.

"I don't understand," sniffed Nat. "You said you change at the full moon, not on a sunny afternoon. You won't shrivel up in the sun, will you?" he added anxiously.

"That's *vampires*," said Woody.

Nat paced up and down, clutching his head with his hands.

"What do we do?" he asked, panicking. "Wha . . . ?"

"*Cloves*. Need cloves," interrupted Woody.

With an enormous effort, Nat pulled himself together and forced a smile. He whipped off his T-shirt and handed it to Woody. "You need *clothes*."

"Yep," said Woody patiently. "'S'what I said."

"Stay here," said Nat firmly. "I'll see what I can do." He patted the top of Woody's arm reassuringly. "And don't worry."

Woody smiled and sat down next to the painted van while Nat scouted the cars to see if any were unlocked. Maybe he would find an old blanket or seat cover that Woody could drape around himself until they got home. *Home!* Nat groaned. How on earth was he going to explain this to his family?

He trudged back to the ring. There was no sign of them anywhere. He knew they wouldn't have gone home, because Mick had wanted to stay for the bands. He was sure Mick wouldn't miss the Wurzels for anything.

He pulled his cap forward. He hoped no one would recognize him as the owner of the hopeful but crazy entrant in "Dog with the Most Appealing Face." As he checked out the area behind the stage for any pieces of clothing that might be useful, he was struck by the music. The band who'd opened the show was playing a kind of country music, full of loud, joyful, funky riffs, and everyone was up and dancing. Nat took a peek at the singer, who was young and strikingly pretty, with fire-engine red hair and an unusual voice. To Nat, it sounded fluid and creamy, like the sound of a violin when it is played very well.

As he walked away from the stage, he noticed a smaller crowd gathered around a group of morris dancers and mimes, who were enacting a scene where someone was being savaged by a person wearing a papier-mâché wolf's head, complete with massive teeth and a malevolent gleam in its eye. It all seemed uncomfortably familiar to Nat. Then he noticed that two of the morris men were changing out of their white trousers and rainbow-colored, ribbon-bedecked waistcoats. Nat moved quickly. While the smaller one wasn't looking, he stole the outfit and threw it behind a large tree.

He lingered near the sideshows, trying to appear non-chalant. When he thought it was safe, he nipped behind the tree and grabbed the stolen morris dancer's outfit.

Back at Woody's hiding place, Woody eyed the costume doubtfully.

"It's all I could get, so put it on. Come ON. Quick!" pleaded Nat. "Before someone sees us."

Woody gave Nat back his T-shirt and put on the shirt and pants, but turned up his nose at the vest.

"Do you feel as though you might change back soon?" asked Nat anxiously.

Woody shook his head. "Sorry," he said miserably.

Nat sat down heavily, wondering what to do next. He nearly jumped out of his skin when he felt a hand on his shoulder. It was his mum.

"*There* you are!" said Jude, looking relieved. "But where's Woody?"

Nat looked around for Woody. *Where on earth had he gone?* He had been there seconds ago.

"I'm . . . I'm not sure," he said, thinking fast. "I think he might have tried to find his way back to Tate's farm or something."

"Doubt it," said Jude. "But are *you* all right?"

"Yeah," said Nat, with a watery grin. "I'm OK. Just a bit worried about Woody." He bit his lip. *Talk about the understatement of the twenty-first century!*

Jude nodded grimly. "Your granddad was going to have a word with that Teddy Davis, but when he saw him, he and his friends made a sharp exit."

"He's decided to make my life a misery," said Nat glumly. "He goes out of his way to call me names and make fun of me."

Jude sighed. "I'm afraid that's probably Granddad's fault," she said, putting her arm around him.

"Why?" asked Nat, surprised.

"You remember that Granddad said he'd had a few words with Teddy Davis?" asked Jude.

Nat nodded, intrigued.

"Well, it was more than a few words," said Jude. "It was more like, as your granddad would say, 'a clip 'round his ear 'ole.' In fact, the way he told it to me, more like two or three 'clips 'round the ear 'ole.'"

Nat was astonished. It was his granddad who, despite

his love for Dirty Harry films, always said, "Violence never solves anything."

"Teddy Davis is what they call in Temple Gurney a *wrong 'un*," said Jude more seriously. "He was setting traps for animals up at the East Wood. Clawed traps: highly illegal and the cruelest traps of all."

Nat shuddered.

"Granddad was in the woods one night last summer," continued Jude, "when he heard screaming: Rabbits scream terribly when they're hurt. He caught Davis red-handed. Since then he steers clear of him. Granddad was worried you would blame him if you knew."

Nat managed a smile. "Sounds as though old Teddy 'The Tiger' deserved more than a few clips 'round the ear 'ole."

"Don't worry." Jude smiled back. "He'll soon tire of you. The less you take the bait, the less fun it'll be for them."

Nat nodded, not entirely convinced. "I'm going to have another look for Woody," he said. "You might as well enjoy the rest of the show."

"He won't have gone back to the Tates'," said Jude. "Anyway, they're gone now; sold the place. Left yesterday, apparently. Are you sure you wouldn't like me to help you look for Woody?"

Nat shook his head firmly. "No, no, I'll be fine!" he said, forcing a laugh.

Jude gave him a concerned look. "Well, if you're sure . . ."

"Positive," said Nat hastily. "Go on. He might even have gone back to Camellia Lane; you know how smart he is."

Jude ruffled his hair. "It'll be all right, Nat, really it will."

Nat had a feeling his mum was saying that to make *herself* feel better, but at least she wasn't going to try to help him find Woody, who Nat hoped was still nearby — with any luck looking like a gangly white dog again.

As soon as Jude had gone back toward the stage area, Woody stepped out from the bushes, smiling weakly. The shock of the last hour was beginning to wear off, and Nat was relieved and delighted to see Woody again, whatever shape he was in. To his surprise he found he didn't want to go home yet.

"There you are!" cried Nat excitedly. "Come on. We might as well make the most of you being on two legs."

But Woody was rooted to the spot. His nostrils were flaring in and out at an alarming rate and disgusting strings of saliva drizzled onto his shirt.

"What's wrong?" asked Nat in alarm. "You're not on the turn again, are you?"

"What's that?" asked Woody, his eyes glazed.

"What's what?" asked Nat.

"That *smell*!" said Woody, as if in a trance. "It's a-*woooo*nderful!"

Nat sniffed the air. Then he grinned. "That'd be the hot dogs."

"I want hot dogs!" said Woody. "Can we? Now?"

"C'mon." Nat grinned.

Several hot dogs later, Nat and Woody joined the evening crowds to watch the rest of the bands. In between the music, fire-eaters, jugglers, and contortionists performed—all of them exotic, wild-looking people. There were shouts and cheers as the band with the red-haired singer Nat had noticed earlier came back onstage. Nat checked the program. The band was called "Crescent and the Howlers."

"She's *soooo* brilliant!" said Nat, pulling Woody to the front of the crowd. Crescent's hair glinted fire in the evening sun as she whirled around, belting out song after song to the audience, who was dancing and singing to the music.

Suddenly Crescent stopped singing. She announced there was to be a five-minute break and left the stage abruptly. Nat was astonished to see her make a beeline for Woody.

Woody pulled at Nat's sleeve; he was worried she had recognized the stolen morris dancer's outfit and wanted it back. But Nat stood firm.

She was even more beautiful close up, thought Nat. The sort of girl Apple would describe as "good-lookin' and she knows it."

Crescent made as if to say something, then looked around furtively, gesturing to the boys to follow her. When they had reached the back of a large truck, she turned to face them.

"Why aren't you with the others?" she asked in hushed tones. Woody stared at the girl, who was, Nat now realized, only about sixteen.

"Oh, no, he's not really a morris dancer," said Nat, trying not to be tongue-tied in the company of such beauty.

The girl ignored him completely. "It's not safe," she continued. "You're barely disguised."

Poor Woody looked bewildered. "Who are you?"

The girl shook her red hair impatiently. "I'm Crescent. I'm a sister."

Woody looked delighted. "My sister?" He launched himself at her, nostrils flaring, rubbing his shaggy head against hers. To Nat's surprise the girl seemed to take all this attention in stride. That is, until Woody licked her face.

"*Eeuw!*" she yelled. "Wolf breath!" She pushed Woody away impatiently. "I'm not *your* sister, silly, I'm *a* sister," she said, wiping Woody's saliva off her face. "Are you going to travel with us or not?"

"I'm confused . . . ," said Woody.

The girl frowned and turned to Nat. "I know what he is," she said, pointing at Woody. "And you should be keeping a closer eye on him," she added bossily. "He shouldn't be out—not like this, in public." She quickly looked behind her. "If you're seen, it could be very dangerous," she said in a hushed voice. "Don't you know *anything*?"

Nat caught his breath. "What d'*you* know?" he challenged.

"I know that people have been asking around, in *our* circles, anyway," she said, turning back to Woody. "It won't be long before they find out you're not dead, you know."

"Not dead?" said Nat in alarm. "Of course he's not dead!"

Crescent eyed him coolly, her lip curled slightly, revealing white teeth.

"You need to get some help," she replied. "This is too much responsibility for a kid your age."

Nat began to feel some of his admiration evaporate. Pretty or not, just who did this girl think she was?

The girl's expression softened momentarily. "Look, I'm sorry. I assumed you had been to see Iona. I thought you must know what was happening."

Nat was fed up with not knowing what was going on, although the name Iona did ring a distant bell.

"Who?" he asked sulkily.

"Iona de Gourney. She's Wiccan."

"What, like Welsh?" asked Nat, puzzled.

"No," snapped Crescent. "Like *Witch*."

Nat closed his eyes. He felt the real world slipping away again.

Woody took charge for the first time. "Why d'you say I should be trav . . . traveling with you?" he asked.

"Because you need to leave this town." Crescent sighed, as if explaining something to a very elderly deaf person. "Before they find out that Tate didn't shoot you."

"Who are 'they'?" asked Nat.

"The government, of course."

"Oh," said Nat, relieved. "That's not so bad. Woody made it sound as though he was being hunted by Very Bad People."

"He is!" spat Crescent.

"But you said . . ." Nat was confused.

Crescent's prickly expression evened out again. "Look, we just got a message to come and play here and pick up a brother so that he could travel safely with us when we tour Eastern Europe."

"How did you know I'm Wolven?" asked Woody.

"Duh!" said Crescent rudely. "Look at the state of your eyebrow. And your dress sense!" Then she smiled. "I lead a normal enough life most of the time." She put her fingers up to her vivid green eyes and deftly extricated colored contact lenses, which, once removed, showed the real color underneath. They were a perfect, jack-o'-lantern orange. Nat gasped, the hair pricking on his arms. *The same color as the creature in his nightmare!* And her eyebrows seemed to be knitting into one, too.

Woody's jaw dropped. "Are you . . . Wolven?"

Crescent laughed and shook her red hair. "Don't you know anything? I'm just a common old werewolf. But you're one of the King's Wolven. You know: fearless, telepathic warriors and all that. I'm talking to a living legend."

"How do you control your changes?" asked Nat, not understanding any of this but still trying to hold on to something useful in the strange conversation. "Because Woody doesn't seem to know when it's going to happen."

Crescent gave him a quick smile. "Practice and patience," she said smugly. "Forget all the stuff you hear about shape-shifting rules — although I admit it is harder to resist the urge when the moon is full. You really need to speak with the lady Iona, she knows far more than . . ." She was interrupted by someone calling her name urgently.

"Gotta go; we're back on. Here, take this." She pressed

a piece of paper into Woody's palm and squeezed his hand between both of hers.

"The lady who? What lady?" asked Nat, still confused.

Crescent grinned. "You'll find out if you go to see her." Then her face became serious again. "We leave next week, after Priddy Fair. If you want to come, I'll meet you at noon at Temple Cross, and you, too." She shot a friendlier look at Nat. "How about it? Want to tour with the best band in Europe?" She blew them both a kiss and, with a whirl of her sequined skirt, she retreated down the dark alley of trucks back to the stage.

Nat and Woody stared at each other. Crescent's information had baffled them even more. One of the King's Wolven? What did she mean? And what's more, Nat noticed that Woody had a soppy lovelorn expression on his face as he watched the rest of the Howlers' set.

When the band had left the stage, Nat glanced at the paper Crescent had given Woody. *Iona de Gourney.* He'd read that name before. Of course! The card from the library. He'd forgotten all about it. He rummaged in the pockets of his jeans and triumphantly pulled out the card, now crumpled and dirty:

That was today. Nat looked at his bare arm, forgetting his watch was no longer there. He strained his head to read the time on the watch of the man next to him. *Seven-thirty*. They'd easily make it to Meade Lodge in time. What a piece of luck they'd met Crescent! Nat shivered. Was it luck, though? Jude would call it Providence, like something was *meant* to be for the best. Whatever it was, it could unlock the mystery of Woody's past—and any chance he had for a future.

CHAPTER 10
MEADE LODGE

The woods, ancient and impenetrable, formed a semicircle of protection around the towns of Temple Gurney and Temple Cross, like the hug of a green-limbed giant. Local guidebooks warned against penetrating the outer rim of the woods to reach its core, unless armed with a machete. What they didn't actually say was that the machete might come in handy to deal with what you might meet inside.

At Jude's insistence, Mick had shown Nat areas of the woods where he could take Woody for safe walks without getting lost. The trees grew sparse and spindly where East Wood met Diamond Bay, as the soil became sandier and thinner, making it difficult for them to thrive. Mick had been very clear that they should never leave the path, and Nat had no intention of disobeying him.

Rumors of government skulduggery still persisted. It was said by the locals that it was impossible to go very deep into the woods, because many of the areas used in the government's shady experiments had been contaminated.

Mick had pooh-poohed any such talk. "There is no contamination," he said bluntly. "They only say that to keep kids out, because it's so dangerous. There's all sorts in them woods, including deep gullies you can fall down. Not to mention the bears."

Nat's eyes had widened at the mention of bears.

"Oh, never mind him!" Apple had said, throwing her husband a look. "The real problem is the time it would take for emergency services to find you if you got lost."

On their way to meet Iona de Gourney, Nat was determined to avoid the woods at all costs, so they came down into the valley from the side nearest the sea. They made for the deserted beach.

Meade Lodge stood alone, well above the shoreline, the many mullioned windows glinting in the evening sun, almost blinding the boys as they ran along the valley. Castellated towers flanked the medieval gatehouse, giving it a fairy-tale appearance — nothing at all like Nat had expected, not that he'd really known what to expect.

The boys hit a problem when they reached the massive

gates. Ivy covered them in thick fronds, making Nat suspect no one had used them for years. There was no visible point of entry, no bell or latch.

"If I had a cell phone, I could call her and tell her we're outside," said Nat, trying in vain to peer over the top of the gates. "How about I give you a leg up? You could see if there's any way to open them from the inside."

Woody looked less than happy with this arrangement. "What if . . . there's something horrible waiting on the other side?" he asked.

By now Nat was tired, worn-out, and about to lose his temper, big-time. "For someone who's supposed to be a fearless fighting machine, or whatever Crescent was ranting on about, you're doing a good impression of the Cowardly Lion," he said.

Woody grinned sheepishly. "Promise you won't leave me?"

Nat promised impatiently. He was just about to hoist Woody upward when he stopped in astonishment. The thick, gnarled fronds of the ivy started to *move*. Slowly but surely, they snaked back, eventually leaving the latch exposed.

"Someone's pulling it!" mouthed Nat to Woody.

With a grating sound that made Nat's teeth hurt and Woody increase his viselike grip on Nat's arm, the gates opened. They were being allowed in.

Nat laughed shakily. Somebody was having a great big fat joke at their expense. And what if there *were* guard dogs? What if Iona de Gourney was watching them as they crept up the sweeping drive? What if she was a bad witch? Nat suddenly wished they hadn't come.

Vast hydrangea bushes the color of oxidized blood flanked the driveway. When they reached the garden, it was so quiet that they were sure Iona de Gourney would know they were there just by hearing them breathe.

"No one else here," whispered Woody nervously. "Just us?"

"Why am I not surprised?" Nat whispered back grimly. "I bet we're the only people invited."

It was peaceful in the garden. Somewhere far off, a lone wood pigeon cooed, and they could hear the low buzz of insects collecting pollen from the many flowers that grew there, their combined scents almost too overpowering in the still evening.

A movement from one of the hydrangea bushes caught Nat's eye and he motioned to Woody to stand still. They held their breath until a beautiful muntjac deer emerged, her two delicate fawns by her side. The doe paused for a moment and gave the boys an inquisitive glance. She sniffed the air when she saw Woody, sensing something different about him. She tensed for a moment, her ears twitching slightly, then appeared to accept both boys as harmless and glided away, her fawns following behind.

To Nat's delight, other animals appeared, as if from nowhere. Rabbits gamboled and bucked, and an elderly badger shambled past, ignoring the boys as it snuffled for food. There were goats and a donkey and, most unexpected of all, a pure white peacock, its plumage exquisite lace. Just as the boys began to relax, the peacock gave a series of terrible cries, like a woman screaming. Woody almost jumped into Nat's arms.

A great black shadow blotted out the sun. It was cold in the shadow, and Nat was scared to look into it, afraid that Iona de Gourney was towering above them in all her terrible glory. He forced himself to look. There in front of them stood an enormous black horse, its head seeming almost as big as Nat's entire body. Nat, who had never had anything to do with horses in his life, stood rooted to the spot, waiting to be trampled under its hooves, which were bigger than dinner plates.

The Goliath horse drew back its top lip, exposing great square teeth that appeared to Nat the size of small gravestones. Then it tossed its head and exhaled gusts of hot air down its nostrils, blowing both Nat's and Woody's hair back from their foreheads. It lowered its head down to Nat's level and blew its nose, leaving bright green skid marks on his white T-shirt. Nat and Woody burst out laughing in delighted disgust.

Still giggling weakly, they reached the huge, studded front door. Nat reached for the old-fashioned bellpull. As his hand touched the rope, the door swung open suddenly, making him jump.

They felt like they'd traveled back in time. The woman who stood in the doorway smiling at the boys, her lovely heart-shaped face framed with masses of long, spirally hair the color of old gold, was dressed in a kind of medieval frock. The only clue she was actually living in the twenty-first century was her bright green nail polish, which exactly matched the color of her eyes. She didn't seem in the least bit surprised to see them, and opened the door wider, smiling first at Nat, then Woody. She spoke, her pleasant voice welcoming and warm.

"Hey, boys," she said. "Crescent told me to expect visitors."

"Oh, wow," breathed Nat, "did she contact you by magic?"

"No, she called me on her cell phone," said Iona, her smile fading a little.

Sensing they had started off on the wrong foot by mentioning magic so early in their acquaintance, Nat tried to make amends. "This is Woody," he said politely. "We've come for your werewolf talk."

Iona held out her arms as if in welcome. Nat watched in amazement as Woody bounded over to Iona, grabbed hold of her, and proceeded to rub his head vigorously against hers, almost knocking her off her feet.

Nat was beside himself with embarrassment. "You're supposed to just shake hands," he hissed, red-faced.

"It's fine." Iona smiled, smoothing her hair. "I'm honored; it shows that he trusts me."

Then she looked at Nat closely, her green eyes bright. "Nathaniel, isn't it?" She didn't wait for his reply. "You know, *werewolf* is a term rarely used nowadays. It isn't really politically correct to call any self-respecting shape-shifter a *were-* anything. You should really call them lycans, which is short for *lycanthropes.*"

Nat swallowed, feeling young and silly.

"Don't worry, Nathaniel," Iona continued, still smiling warmly. "You can't be expected to know everything; that's why you've come, yes?"

Nat nodded politely. He supposed being called Nathaniel was better than Natalie.

Iona stood back to allow them through the ancient door.

"Come on in, you two." She smiled encouragingly. "We have an awful lot to get through."

Nat hesitated. This woman *looked* nice enough, but his parents had always warned him about Stranger Danger. He was pretty sure if Iona de Gourney turned out to be a "wrong 'un," their only hope would be if Woody could turn into a Wolven very quickly.

He took a deep breath as the two of them crossed the threshold and followed Iona through the flagged passage into a room that must once have been a great banquet hall. It was furnished in rich reds, earthy ochers, and autumn browns, while the soft velvet throws on the sofas were various shades of green: sage, emerald, and a deep jade similar in hue to Iona de Gourney's eyes. And the smell! Although the room was cool for such a hot summer's evening, the spicy scents of ginger, chili, and paprika, combined with the boys' own excited anticipation, made the air around them feel charged.

A large Siamese cat artistically draped over an armchair cracked open a sapphire blue eye as they walked in. "Meet Clawdia," said Iona, gesturing to the cat. The cat chose not to acknowledge Nat and Woody. Another Siamese cat lay asleep in the hearth. Nat knelt down to stroke it. *Ugh!* He pulled his hand away quickly; it was as hard as a rock!

"Stuffed," said Iona by way of an explanation. "That's Trinny, Clawdia's predecessor."

The quietness was almost unbearably loud, despite a low hum—the kind of noise you sometimes hear when you are close to telephone poles. It took Nat a few seconds before he realized the buzz was coming from a number of very expensive-looking computers at the far end of the extraordinary room. "Hasn't anyone else turned up for the lecture?" gabbled Nat, knowing the answer.

Iona grinned. But it was a nice grin, not crafty or threatening. Nat relaxed.

"The card *was* just for you," she confirmed. "A nice touch, don't you think?"

"But how did you know . . . ?"

"Call it a woman's intuition. I just planted it when the librarian wasn't looking."

Nat thought about it for a moment. He was certain Iona de Gourney had not been anywhere in the library: She was pretty noticeable. But he forgot this for now as he breathed in the room's wonderful smell; he had never been anywhere like this before. The sections of the walls that were not taken up by hundreds of leather-bound books were covered with beautiful tapestries of unicorns, jousting knights, castles, and what looked to Nat like coats of arms. They all seemed very old, like the Bayeux Tapestry, which his mum and dad had taken him to see last year.

"Help yourself," invited Iona, gesturing to the shelves. "Come on, Woody. You can help me in the kitchen while Nat browses."

Itching with curiosity, Nat reached up and pulled out a volume entitled *The Time Traveler's Compendium to Edible Fungus*. A quick look inside proved to be boring but quite disgusting in parts. A book with a lurid cover featuring shrunken heads was entitled *Who Do Voodoo?* by someone with the unlikely pseudonym of I. Smallhead. Another was called *Faerie Magick*: Yuck, that sounded girlie! He scanned the rest. On the lower shelves were books with titles like: *Doppelgängers, Are You Who You Think You Are?* and *Cutlery Bending with the Mind — Is There Ever Really a Point?*

When Iona and Woody returned, Nat was engrossed in *Blood & Guts Volume II: The Role of the Lycanthrope in Her Majesty's Service.*

"Are there really werew — lycanthropes in the army?" he asked Iona, his eyes wide.

"Only in the Special Air Service," said Iona briskly, handing Nat a glass of pinkish liquid. "But never mind that just now. I've something special for you, something which will help you understand Woody far better than any old talk on lycans can."

She pointed to the large refectory table at the end of the room where Woody was carefully setting down a small tray. Looking out of place among all the ancient artifacts, the large table was set up with the state-of-the-art computers and electronic equipment that Nat had heard humming earlier. Close up, they looked even more impressive.

"Not bad, huh?" said Iona, amused at the boys' reverent expressions. "But that's not what I want to show you. *This* is why I asked you here."

Iona's voice betrayed her excitement as she placed a large book in front of the boys.

Nat felt his heart miss a beat. The book looked ancient, as though, like Iona, it belonged in another time. He couldn't wait to see what it contained, only just resisting the urge to snatch it from Iona's hands. The faded leather cover was embossed with an elaborate gold design on the front, which glittered subtly in the dim light. The title was almost indecipherable; then Nat realized in disappointment that it was written in French. (His French was pretty bad.)

"These," said Iona proudly, "are the original chronicles of my ancestor, Sir William de Gourney, the very same man whom Temple Gurney is named after. William was a Knight Templar, part of an elite band of warrior monks; I suppose you could describe them as a sort of medieval special forces."

"Cool," murmured Nat, still not knowing where this was leading.

"Nine centuries ago, Sir William journeyed to the Holy Land in the company of King Richard . . ."

"The Lionheart!" gasped Nat.

". . . on the Third Crusade." Iona nodded, smiling. "Sir William completed the writings when his crusading days were over. The chronicle disappeared about a hundred years later, along with the Templar gold and other priceless treasures."

Nat whistled. "We did a school project about the Templars," he said. "When the Crusades lost everyone's support, the fighting monks weren't needed anymore and turned into bankers."

"Sort of," Iona conceded, still smiling. "Two centuries after they were formed, the Knights Templar were accused of terrible crimes against God, and hounded into exile. Hundreds were tortured and burned, but many managed to escape and existed in underground movements."

"But what will that tell us about the Wolven?" asked Nat.

"Well, Nathaniel, the title of the chronicle is *Journeys with the King's Wolven*," said Iona softly.

Nat almost shook with excitement. *The King's Wolven?* Wasn't that what Crescent had called Woody at the fair?

Iona gave Nat some thin white gloves to put on. "Do try your rose hip cordial, Nat," she urged. "Best finish it before you read the manuscript."

Nat winced at the thought of spilling something on the ancient document. The drink was wonderful, like nothing he had ever tasted before. He drained it thirstily and put the empty glass on the tray.

"You'll probably find the text difficult to read," Iona continued, lighting one of the lamps, "but Sir William was an excellent artist, too. I think you'll find his pictures quite illuminating."

Nat sat at the table, anxious to get started. Iona was right; the ancient writing would have been hard enough to follow in English, let alone French. The words were hand-written in the same fancy script as the cover, and after a while, they seemed to merge together, making Nat's eyes sting. The spicy smell in the room seemed to be stronger, and now he could feel his eyes droop. His arms and legs felt so weak that he wouldn't have been able to move them even if he'd wanted to. Eventually, he stopped trying to read and concentrated instead on the expertly drawn pictures. It was almost impossible to believe they had been created nine hundred years ago; the colors glowed vibrantly as Nat became lost in Sir William's story. He could imagine riding through the Holy Land with Richard the Lionheart as he led his army forward. He could almost smell the sea as Sir William rode along the strange, foreign coast, so different from the one he knew there in the southwest of England. When he reached a particularly lifelike picture of the Lionheart inspecting the dead and dying on the battlefield, a lump rose in his throat and he felt he could actually hear the terrible screams of the wounded horses. He was so engrossed, he was only half aware that his chair was swaying, making him shift from side to side, threatening to tip him off.

It was making him feel sick. *Ugh!* He felt terrible. He burped loudly and tasted rose hip again. He shut his eyes for a second. A weird noise invaded his ears; it reminded him of the peal a glass makes when you rub your wet finger around its rim. The sound quickly reached an almost unbearable pitch, and then there was nothing but clammy darkness. Nat felt a horrible sucking sensation in his stomach, as though he was being vacuumed out of the world, and then he felt nothing.

CHAPTER 11

THE KING'S WOLVEN

When it was light again, Nat slowly opened his eyes.

At first, his vision was blurred and the light was almost too bright to bear. He was uncomfortably hot and thirsty. He tried licking his lips to moisten them, but his tongue felt blistered and useless. Still dimly aware of the swaying motion, he plucked up the courage to look down.

He was no longer sitting on a chair in the safety of Iona's gracious medieval hall: He was sitting astride a great big black horse!

Nat looked around him in confusion as his vision cleared. He was surrounded by other horses ridden by men who at first glance appeared to be wearing touristy British flag T-shirts and ski masks. *What on earth was going on?*

And no wonder he was so hot. Underneath his own England T-shirt was a weird metallic type of vest. His pants were made of the same stuff and his sword was chafing against his leg. . . . *Sword?* Then it hit him: By some powerful force of magic or hypnotic state, he had been transported back through time!

What Nat had mistaken for men in England T-shirts were living, breathing medieval Knights Templar, just like those in Sir William de Gourney's chronicle. Nat glanced nervously to his left. The rider closest to him had been wounded. He was slumped forward on the neck of his warhorse, barely able to hold on. To Nat's right, his neighbor wore a grim expression and a circlet of gold on his head. His horse was a stunning white charger and his shield a brilliant red with a gold design. It was the shield that helped Nat realize whose company he shared. For embossed on the gold and the red of St. George's cross were three lions. *Three lions!*

Nat didn't know much about the Crusades, but he knew about the three lions. Toward the end of his crusading days, King Richard I, "the Lionheart," had adopted three lions on a red background for his seal and coat of arms. Nat glanced again at the man who rode an arm's length away from him. *It was impossible, wasn't it? But,* thought Nat, *if I've been transported back through time to experience this, anything's possible!* He was positive that the owner of the shield was Richard the Lionheart, and somehow, Nat found himself riding alongside him on the Third Crusade! Rigid with fear, he wondered what would happen if they were ambushed again, like he'd seen in Sir William's chronicle, and he had to fight.

They rode in grim silence apart from the occasional snorting of the horses and the muffled sound of their hooves on the sandy ground. As the shadows lengthened and the horses got their second wind, Nat found he could control his mount with ease, and he managed to stay on at a gallop without dropping his sword or shield. As he rode, the horse's hooves beat a tattoo on the sand and Nat felt himself settle into the smooth rhythm.

Memories that were not his own flashed into Nat's brain. Somehow, the chronicle had helped him to share all the memories and experiences Sir William de Gourney had recorded. He even knew that the mighty black horse he rode was named Arcadia.

How did I know that? thought Nat, amazed at the flood of information. *It's like I've* become *Sir William!*

Then Nat had his first comforting thought. *If I have some-how been transported into Sir William's body, I'll be safe. After all, he must have survived the Crusade to write this chronicle.*

Nat and the crusaders journeyed north under the for-eign sky for what seemed like hours. When darkness fell, the company stopped to water their horses. The tempera-ture dropped sharply and the wind picked up, gathering speed as it raced through the hills. Nat's bravery disinte-grated when, through the eerie thrumming of the wind, wild, whooping howls could be heard—faint at first, then becoming louder as they drew closer.

Then the howls stopped. Whatever had made the noise was hidden in the trees. Nat could bear it no longer; he lifted his right arm experimentally, bringing up the sword in his hand. To his amazement, thirty or forty of his fel-low crusaders did the same.

"Stay your weapons!" snarled King Richard. Nat real-ized that the Lionheart had given the order in French, a language that Nat struggled with at school, and yet he had understood every word. He copied the other men as they sheathed their swords. They seemed to be waiting

for something. But what? Nat shivered and shook in anticipation.

And then, in the distance, came the reward for their patience. By squinting his eyes against the velvety-dark night, Nat could make out tiny lights shining through the mist. Everyone watched, mesmerized by the phenomenon, many exclaiming with childish delight. Nat, too, felt himself relax as he watched the patterns of light grow, until several pairs of floating jewels shone out, their warm topaz glow lending a welcome heat to the cold night. As the last of the mist retreated back into the soil, the strange visitors were revealed at last.

In the stark new light of the enormous moon, with their gossamer-white fur shimmering silver and their strange topaz eyes shining like beacons, stood a company of twelve magnificent wolves. Nat watched in wonder; their resemblance to Woody was striking. One by one, they moved forward toward the king, so close to Nat that he could feel their hot breath on his leg. They bowed low, gracefully and reverently. Nat watched, breath held, as the Lionheart smiled—an enormous, triumphant grin, his teeth startlingly white in his battle-grimed face. Laughing and whooping, he punched the night sky with a victorious fist.

"Thank God and St. George!"

The Wolven pack responded by howling joyfully, threatening to burst Nat's eardrums. The horses were jostling, the knights and foot followers were cheering, making Nat feel dizzy again. He sensed himself slithering bonelessly from Arcadia, blood pounding in his ears, heart fluttering. Feeling the hot breath of one of the Wolven on his face, he panicked, and put out his hand instinctively to push it away. He needed some air, but was surrounded by concerned furry bodies. Then he felt himself falling into a dark tunnel, until at last he was aware of nothing.

Seconds later, Nat found himself on the floor of the banquet hall, retching violently and wracked with sickness. It was at least five minutes before he was able to sit up. He was aware of the concerned voices of Iona and Woody, and gradually his head stopped buzzing.

Despite the lingering dizziness, Nat was bursting with questions about his flip back to the past: Had he actually traveled, *disappeared*? Had he really inhabited the body of Sir William de Gourney, or had the rose-colored drink Iona had given him contained some sort of mind-altering magic? *That would definitely be illegal!* He tried to get up, but his legs, still rubbery and uncooperative, let him down. Iona and Woody helped him struggle to his feet, their faces almost comically concerned.

"Welcome back," said Iona.

"You could have warned me!" said Nat shakily. "Was it that drink or Sir Will's chronicle that made me feel so ill?"

Iona looked puzzled. "The book is enchanted, but it's completely harmless—it's what we call an *enabler*. It helps readers open their minds far enough for them to be able to travel as far into the past or present as they need to. It's so much easier than reading. But Nat, you weren't in any danger, I promise. The drink I gave you was a veloc-ity antidote; it's supposed to *stop* you from feeling travel sickness."

"Well, it didn't work," said Nat resentfully.

"Hot dogs . . . at the fair!" cried Woody. "We had five with chili sauce! Must have been them."

"Ugh, *shut up*," said Nat weakly.

"No harm done, Nat," soothed Iona. "You're back safely."

"So did I actually *travel*, then?" asked Nat. "Did . . . did I actually *disappear*?"

"You did!" Iona laughed. "Brilliant, isn't it?"

A big, fat grin appeared on Nat's face. He was way too excited to remain annoyed with Iona. She had, after all, shown him things that were so incredible he knew he would never forget them as long as he lived.

"I wish you could have been there," said Nat excitedly. "I saw the Wolven and Richard the Lionheart and . . ."

"I *did* see it," said Woody. "I saw it . . . through you."

"But . . . ?" asked Nat, bewildered. "Oh! *Oooh* . . . you read my mind?"

"You don't . . . you don't mind, do you?" asked Woody anxiously.

"It is all pretty weird," said Nat uncertainly.

"Everything you just experienced happened nine centuries ago," said Iona. "Long before that, in the early dark ages, a lost legend told of golden-eyed white wolves 'fleet of mind and foot' who could change 'smooth of cheek' by the moon's full light. For six centuries they served their kings loyally, appearing whenever they were needed, drifting away like smoke when the job was done. According to Sir William de Gourney's chronicle, the Wolven rarely killed an enemy of the king. Just the sight of them, eyes flashing, teeth bared, was enough to send them running for the hills!"

"They came to help," said Nat. "When I saw them, they had come to escort Richard to safety. It was like he was expecting them."

"It was their job," said Iona simply.

"But what happened to the Wolven clans after the Crusades?" asked Nat. "Did they go into hiding like the Knights Templar?"

"Times were changing," said Iona. "Life had become safer and strong magic was dying. After two hundred years of conflict and a terrible loss of human lives, the Crusades at last came to an end."

Woody's lip curled. "Bad," he said. "Crusades were bad."

"We know that now," agreed Iona, "but in those days life was very different: brutal and short. If the kings of the time declared war, their subjects had no choice but to follow. After the last Crusade, in gratitude for their loyal service to the Crowns of England, the Wolven were guaranteed safe passage for the rest of their lives. They were absorbed into the woods and the forests, living as wolves, preferring a simpler life. Then all knowledge of them died, and they became the stuff of legend only; stories passed down from generation to generation, gradually fading away. And now, I have a living, breathing legend sitting on my sofa!"

"But what *now*?" asked the living, breathing legend. "Crescent told us . . . you know who's hunting me?"

Iona went pale. "What do you know about Proteus?" she asked.

"Nothing," admitted Nat, "apart from the fact that Woody has it tattooed on the back of his neck."

"Is Proteus c . . . coming to get me?" Woody's voice quaked.

"Proteus isn't a man," said Iona grimly. "Proteus is a *government project*."

CHAPTER 12
THE PROTEUS FILES

"The original Proteus project was just a study program," explained Iona, pouring tea from a delicate china teapot. "Help yourselves, boys," she added, gesturing to the delicious-looking pile of sandwiches and cakes she had put on the table.

Nat dug Woody in the ribs. "Saliva check," he hissed.

"'Scuse me?" asked Woody, eyeing the food hungrily.

"You're *drooling*," said Nat, hoping Iona hadn't noticed the strings of dribble threatening to drop onto her sofa.

"The project studied shape-shifting beings," Iona went on. "Werewolves, as you would call them. It examined men, and very occasionally women, who were afflicted by lycanthropy, which, as you know, is the ability to change into wolves."

"So what has it got to do with Woody?" asked Nat, helping himself to a piece of cake. "He's not a werewolf."

"The head of the project was a man named Professor Robert Paxton, a brilliant scientist who had devoted his life to studying shape-shifting beings. Years ago, when I became involved with Proteus, I shared his fascination with the legend of the King's Wolven. Sir William's chronicle helped us to locate them."

Woody, who had been sniffing each individual sandwich, stopped abruptly. "You found my . . . clan?"

Iona nodded. "Professor Paxton spent several months with them, and learned that everything Sir William had written was true. Then he made a terrible mistake. He brought the younger members of the clan here to Somerset, to Helleborine Halt, where they agreed to be studied for one month only."

"And he went back on his word?" guessed Nat.

"No!" said Iona, shaking her head vehemently. "The Wolven were betrayed by a man named Dr. Gabriel Gruber."

"Never heard of him," said Nat, with his mouth full. "Is he the one looking for Woody?"

Iona got up from the sofa. "Among others," she said mysteriously. "I'll show you."

"It's not another trip back in time, is it?" groaned Nat, holding his bulging stomach. "I've just eaten three pieces of cake."

"No magic needed," said Iona, "not this time."

The boys followed her as she positioned herself at one of the computers. Her fingers flew expertly across the keyboard, a small frown of concentration creasing her brow. Random data scrolled down the screen for a few seconds, then — success! PROTEUS popped up on the screen, complete with a howling wolf logo.

"You *work* for them?" asked Nat.

Iona shook her head. "I used to," she said, still frowning slightly. "Three years ago, Professor Paxton disappeared and I was 'no longer required.'"

"But what . . . why . . . ?" stammered Nat.

"Shhhh, I'll get to that in a moment," she said. "Since my dismissal, I've been hacking into the Proteus files. I made these images from security camera footage at Helleborine Halt." She turned to Woody. "These are the people who betrayed the clan and who will stop at nothing to find you."

A color image of an immaculately dressed man came into view.

"This is Dr. Gabriel Gruber," said Iona grimly. "One of Harvard University's finest. He's a great example of the fact that looks can be deceptive; he's absolutely stark *barking* mad. Dr. Gruber tricked Professor Paxton into telling him about the Wolven study. Not only that, he persuaded the Special Weapons Division that he could create an indestructible telepathic band of mercenaries: you know, soldiers who will fight for money, not because they care which side they're on. To do this, he planned to combine the DNA of the superintelligent and telepathic Wolven with the cunning and near-immortality of the werewolf."

She clicked onto the site again. "And this drop-dead gorgeous specimen is Lucas Scale."

Nat and Woody both recoiled in horror. Grinning straight at them, orange eyes glowing malevolently, was the creature from Nat's nightmare.

"*Nooo* . . . it can't be . . ." Nat shuddered, all the color draining from his face. "That's the wolf thing in the woods—from my nightmare."

Iona's eyes widened. "You have dreams about Lucas Scale?"

Nat nodded. "My mum told me there's no such thing as monsters, but it's not true, is it?"

"Scale was human once," said Iona. "He was bitten by one of the Halt werewolves; he tried to reverse the contamination, but it went wrong halfway through and his condition is deteriorating."

"But how come *I* had a nightmare about him?" asked Nat, puzzled. "It's Woody he wants, not me."

"As Scale becomes more wolf than man, his enhanced senses will tell him that Woody is still near," explained Iona. "He isn't strong enough yet to target a specific telepathic subject, but he's getting better all the time. It won't be long before he gets lucky."

To Nat's relief, the image of Lucas Scale was replaced by another: two enormous men in polarized glasses.

"The Spaghetti twins," announced Iona. "Scale recruited them as werewolves himself, both at the same time. Two for the price of one, you might say."

"BOGOF!" cried Woody.

"I beg your pardon?" said Iona, raising her eyebrows.

"You *buy* one, you get one *free*," said Woody in a Scottish accent.

Nat couldn't help grinning. "It's from a TV commercial for two-ply toilet paper. He needs to get out more."

Iona's eyebrows returned to their proper position. "The Spaghetti brothers are Gruber's general gophers and bodyguards."

"I wouldn't like to bump into them on a dark night." Nat shuddered.

"There's something else I need to show you," said Iona. She hesitated, glancing at Woody. "The Wolven files."

Woody's eyes flashed excitedly. "Can we see now?" he pleaded. "Please, Iona?"

Nat felt uncomfortable. There was something in Iona's voice that warned him it was not going to be easy viewing.

Iona bit her lip. "The experiments to create a hybrid between the Wolven and the werewolves failed spectacularly. Their blood was incompatible; any offspring died shortly after birth. The werewolves became more and more unpredictable and unstable. Several very bad things happened that were covered up; some local children disappeared, and Professor Paxton was blamed. The Wolven were too sick to be of any further use, and the government back at Whitehall ordered the project to be scaled down. Gabriel Gruber escaped with just a warning, but Professor Paxton was discredited, his life's work destroyed. Shortly after Woody was born, the professor disappeared." Iona scrolled down and clicked on a folder labeled "Highly Classified." She double-clicked on it while Nat and Woody held their breath.

A video file opened with a shot of a walled garden.

Woody gasped audibly as a dozen pure white Wolven came into view, followed by a smiling Iona and a tall, slightly stooped man who Nat guessed must be Professor Paxton.

"Look at them," marveled Nat. "Woody, they're your clan."

Woody turned to Iona. "They . . . are they . . . all dead?" he asked very quietly.

Iona's green eyes brimmed with tears. "I don't know for certain," she admitted shakily. "This video was shot just before Gruber took control. When things went wrong, the professor managed to smuggle you out, Woody, a tiny pup. The work I had done at Proteus was discredited along with his, and I was lucky not to have been involved in an 'accident.' I have no idea if any of the other Wolven were saved."

"Is that how Woody wound up with the Tates?" asked Nat.

Iona nodded. "The professor's cousin, Ophelia Tate, agreed to hide him for a short while. Unfortunately, the professor disappeared before he could make any proper arrangements, so they had to keep him far longer than they had intended. Woody grew up fast and became more difficult to hide. Then the money dried up, and Alec Tate was terrified someone from the Halt would come looking. He was scared of Woody, too. He never did understand that he wasn't dangerous."

"Why didn't you go to the police about Proteus?" asked Nat incredulously.

"I tried," said Iona. "Don't forget this was a top secret project. No living person outside of the government had any idea that shape-shifting beings really existed. Lucas Scale made it very clear that if I took evidence to the newspapers, the professor would be fed to the werewolves, piece by piece."

"Holy mackerel," murmured Nat.

Iona flicked through the Wolven files and the film footage of crazed wolf-men pacing manically in their tiny cells. Worst of all were the mysterious pods hanging in subterranean caves, containing the failed end products of Gruber's hideous experiments. When at last it was over, the boys sat in stunned silence, shaken and horrified by Gruber's cruelty.

"That is why you need to leave," said Iona gently.

"But I don't know where to go," protested Woody.

"You remember Crescent's offer?" asked Iona. "You must leave with the Howlers at the start of their Eastern European tour."

"But Crescent is a *werewolf*," said Nat uncomfortably. "Isn't she . . . er . . . *dangerous*?"

"She can be," agreed Iona, "but like most werewolves she's a creature who just likes to run with the moon. Usually they hunt and eat wild animals like rabbits and deer. Unless they get a taste for human blood, like the poor creatures at the Halt."

"What ha . . . happens then?" asked Woody, trembling.

"Then they are cursed, and no cure can save them," said Iona gravely. "But don't worry, Crescent isn't like them; she is clever when it comes to fading into the background, and she's happy for you to join her."

Woody shook his head. "Don't want to, not on my own."

Nat remained silent. He knew Iona was right, yet he didn't want to say good-bye to Woody.

"Nat comes, too?" said Woody.

Nat shook his head regretfully. "I can't. I can't leave my mum."

"Then I'm not going," said Woody firmly.

"If you stay with Nat, you are both in danger," said Iona. "Any unexpected change, like today's little adventure at the carnival, will definitely attract unwanted attention."

"Will I ever be able to control my change?" asked Woody.

Iona nodded. "It won't be long before you will have complete control; it gets easier the more you change."

"I don't want to go with Crescent," repeated Woody gloomily, "but I don't want to put Nat or his family in danger."

"Scale will catch you if you stay," said Iona firmly.

Suddenly, Nat sprang up. "What time is it? My mum'll be back from the fair by now and wondering where I am."

"Relax," soothed Iona. "It's nine thirty. Your folks won't be home for another hour, which gives you plenty of time."

Nat was astounded. Surely it was later than that? It seemed they had been at Iona's for hours and hours.

"Time passes differently when you flip," said Iona, standing up and walking toward the great oak door. "By the time you get home, Woody will have turned back to Wolven. If you won't change your minds about joining the Howlers, stay out of sight, lie low for the rest of the weekend, and come back on Monday." As Woody and Nat stepped out into the garden, she stood in the open doorway, leaving them with one last thought:

"Then I'll show you some real magic."

CHAPTER 13
LEARNING TO HOWL

"Get ready to jump back off the road if we see any cars," Nat told Woody breathlessly as they hurried along the shadowy perimeter of the wood. He was conscious that even by twilight, *especially* by twilight, Woody would attract unwelcome attention. The morris costume had already split in several places and tufts of white hair poked through the holes.

When the boys reached the shelter of the little beach, with its scrawny growth of trees, Nat heaved a sigh of relief. He glanced sideways at Woody, wishing his change would hurry up and complete. *At least he can still walk*, thought Nat gratefully, remembering the episode at the fair. He hoped he would never have to witness *that* little horror show again.

Nat's head was reeling from all the events of the day. He was still excited about his flip into the past and the few hours when he had been in the company of Richard the Lionheart. It was clear that Woody didn't share his excitement. In fact, he seemed barely interested, and told Nat so.

"What do you mean? This is your *heritage*!" cried Nat, shocked. "How can you say you aren't interested? This is *ginormous*."

Woody shook his head impatiently. "The olden days are gone now!" he cried. "The fighting was bad, and the Cru . . . Crusades were bad, too."

Nat was astonished; he'd never seen Woody quite so upset before.

But Woody hadn't finished. "And ima . . . imagine if you were the last human."

Nat's excitement shriveled up and died. He tried to imagine what it would be like without his mum and dad and Apple and Mick, or anyone human, like him. He felt terrible. Poor Woody had just learned from Iona de Gourney how his clan had been betrayed and suffered horribly.

"What if there are Wolven in other parts of the world?" said Nat, desperate to make amends. "Iona and Professor

Paxton brought your clan over from France. It's possible. We don't even know they all died. Maybe some of them escaped?"

"Then why can't I . . . *feel* them?" asked Woody miserably.

"Maybe because France is off your telepathic radar?" said Nat, trying to coax his friend out of his sad mood.

"S'pose," agreed Woody reluctantly.

"Can you still howl when you're this shape?" asked Nat suddenly.

"'Course," said Woody, puzzled by the question. "Why?"

"Would you teach me?" asked Nat. "You never know, it might come in handy one day."

Woody looked at him sideways, then grinned unnervingly. A little shiver ran down Nat's spine. Woody looked really weird at this halfway point, neither boy nor Wolven.

"Like we could howl . . . to each other?" asked Woody.

Nat nodded enthusiastically. "Yeah, you never know, it might be useful. If you can't talk, maybe I could learn to howl!"

"OK." Woody sighed doubtfully. "But you've got to take it . . . er . . . seri . . ."

"Seriously!" finished Nat. "I will, I will. You go first, if you like."

"Let me get comfortable first."

They sat down on top of one of the stone picnic tables overlooking Diamond Bay.

Woody threw his head back. His powerful throat filled with oxygen. He closed his eyes, and let rip. The phenomenal noise filled the evening sky, bouncing off the quartz-encrusted cliffs surrounding the bay.

It was Nat's turn. He stood on the stone table with his legs apart. He lowered his head backward, as he had seen Woody do.

"UUUrrr."

"What was that?" asked Woody incredulously.

Nat collapsed in a fit of embarrassed giggles.

"No, really, what was it?" asked Woody, concerned. "D'you still feel sick?"

"No," said Nat indignantly, "I just feel a bit self-conscious, that's all. Could you look away?"

He took some deep breaths, flung his head back, and cupped his hands around his mouth. *"AAAoo!"*

Nat finished by pretending to have a coughing fit, to hide his inadequacy.

Woody looked embarrassed for him. "I looked away that time. Still lame."

"Right then." Nat stood up and threw out his chest, his self-consciousness vanishing. *"OOOoooooooahhOOOOh!"* Weak but willing, he gave it his best shot. His eyes watered, his throat was raw.

Woody grinned toothily. "My turn."

Almost in full Wolven form now, he stood on top of the stone table and let another one go. This time, the glass in the bus shelter vibrated and threatened to crack.

Eerily, the echo came back across the bay. When his ears had stopped their painful ringing, Nat gave him a round of applause.

"Who's this an impression of?" asked Nat. He tried to arrange his features into a vampiric leer. In a heavily accented growl, he spoke the words of one of the most feared monsters in literature: *"Listen to them, my children of the night, what music they make."*

Woody cocked his wolfish head to one side.

"Hurry up!" shouted Nat. "You won't be able to speak soon!"

"Er . . . is it the man from up the road, who helped Mick repair the lawnmower?" asked Woody. "The one with the shoes that look like dirty hamburgers?"

Nat frowned. "Shoes like hamburgers? No, you dope, it was *Count Dracula*."

Woody looked hurt.

"Sorry, I forgot," said Nat, mentally kicking himself for being so stupid and insensitive again. How on earth would Woody know that? Most of Woody's education had come from TV game shows and soap operas. "Look, don't worry," Nat continued. "When things calm down a bit, I'll teach you to read properly. We could go to the movies and we can . . ."

Woody interrupted him. "Thanks," he said softly, "but that's normal for *people*. Not *Wolven*."

Nat didn't reply. He realized that what Iona had said had been true. It was madness for Woody to stay in Temple Gurney.

"*AAAAAOOOOOOOOOOOHHHHAAAAAAOOO OOWWW!*"

Woody and Nat froze. This time, it was no echo. The howling was coming from across the valley, from the western side of the wood . . .

From Helleborine Halt.

Woody sniffed the air. "Wolf."

"What if it's that mutant werewolf?" Nat panicked. "What was his name . . . Scale? The one Iona told us about, the one in my nightmare?"

The howling seemed far away, but how long would it take the owner of the howl to catch up with them? Nat had no wish to find out, and although in Wolven form Woody was braver than a lion, he wasn't ready to meet the creature from Nat's nightmare, either. As they raced from the beach, Nat found himself being overtaken. Woody was back on four legs, the last shreds of the morris dancer's costume streaming out behind him as they ran for home.

Nat had hoped his family would still be at the fairground, but as he and Woody slunk through the back door, he could hear raised voices in the garden. Two of the voices belonged to Mick and Jude. But there was another voice, one he couldn't identify at first.

He crept over to the open window. Here he was again, listening when he shouldn't have been. He could see Mick sitting on the swing seat with Apple and Jude, but there was a fourth figure in the garden. A figure in a familiar blue uniform with three stripes on the shoulder. Nat beckoned to Woody, who hauled himself up from the tiles and padded over to the window.

"What you've got to understand, Mick," said the man in the uniform, "is that a big dog like that doesn't just damage property, like the exhibits he wrecked. If he was to bite someone, well, that 'ud be it, really. Gert big German shepherd can cause horrific injuries to someone, 'specially a kid, like."

"Ar," agreed Mick. "No one was hurt, though, Bill, and I did agree to pay for the damage."

Sergeant Beechgood had just finished his shift and was enjoying a glass of Apple's organic brew, with a good wedge of her ripest cheese. From the snippet of conversation Nat had heard, it sounded as though someone had made a complaint. Bill Beechgood continued his lecture.

"And you don't want to be making an enemy of Davis. His father's one of them Masons. Owns a lot of land around Temple Gurney."

"He wasn't bitten," protested Jude, laughter in her voice, "just a bit hot after running such a long way."

Nat didn't smile. It would have been funny if he hadn't seen that terrible gleam of intent in Woody's eyes when he caught up with Teddy.

"Look, Bill, I know you have a job to do, but that Davis kid is a no-good," said Apple with feeling. "It's him you should go and see. He's the one who causes all the problems in the village. He's the one who I've seen bullying and smoking and worse. He ought to be given one of those Anti-Social Behavior Orders, ASBOs."

The sergeant sighed heavily. "This isn't official, but just keep your eye on that dog. P'raps you could get your Nat to take him to training classes or summat?"

There were vague murmurings from the other adults in the garden. Nat let his breath out in relief. More laughter followed, and he hoped the serious stuff was over. He heard the sergeant open the creaky front gate as he took his leave. "By the way, Mick, I hope you haven't been using a hose. I noticed 's mornin' your grass looks a bit special."

Nat could hear his mum laughing, and realized it was the first time he had heard her laugh, really laugh, for weeks; maybe she'd had some good news from Dad.

Mick came into the kitchen and jumped when he saw Nat sitting at the table with a glass of milk.

"How long have you been sat there?" he asked.

"Ages," said Nat soggily, through a milk mustache.

"You found him, then?" Mick said, nodding toward Woody, who lay dozing on the floor.

"Yeah, he was hiding under a truck," said Nat. "He was a bit frightened."

"Not as frightened as that Davis kiddie." Mick grinned. "His dad's complained to Bill Beechgood about what happened. Best try to keep a low profile for the next couple of days."

Nat smiled wearily; Iona had used exactly the same words.

And for two days, it worked.

CHAPTER 14
GONE TO GROUND

Nat Carver looked longingly at his comfy bed as he changed into his pajamas. Even his teeth felt tired, so he didn't bother brushing them. But as soon as his weary head met the pillow, his brain left the town called "Exhaustion" and entered the more hostile territory of "Can't-Get-to-Sleepsville," a place he had often found himself since Lucas Scale had crept uninvited into his dreams. Lying awake with the annoying whirring of the electric fan threatening to drive him crazy, Nat wished he could share his fears with Woody. But Woody lay on his striped blanket under the stars, dreaming of a long-ago clan of brave Wolven.

By five A.M., when the first slivers of sunlight from the east squeezed through the blinds in his bedroom, Nat was in a deep sleep at last. He awoke much later to the smell of toast and bacon and the sound of Apple's infectious laughter. With the arrival of the sun, he found some of his courage had returned, along with his appetite. He dragged on some clothes and bounded downstairs, his belly making weird *boinging* noises in anticipation of breakfast.

His family was already at the table, watching the local morning news show.

"Wonder if they'll have anything on about the fair," said Mick, pouring his tea into his saucer.

Nat smiled weakly. *I seriously hope not*, he thought.

"Aye, aye, here we go," said Mick excitedly. "*Hoo hoo! There I am!*"

The camera had caught the mood of the evening perfectly: everyone singing and dancing and having a wonderful hoedown with the Wurzels. Nat grinned fondly at the sight of his granddad in his eye-wateringly colorful clothes standing at the very front of the crowd, playing air fiddle. The television segment was mainly about the record-breaking attendance and, to Nat's relief, mentioned nothing about the chaos during the dog show. Mick was tickled four shades of pink to see himself on TV, and had to be physically restrained by Apple from telephoning all his friends from the Slaughtered Sheep.

According to the weather forecast, the summer was officially the hottest on record, and there was still no end in sight to the heat wave. In the comforting presence of his family, Nat felt that, for the moment, they were safe. He watched Woody in the garden, snapping lazily at dragon-flies as they flitted in and out of Nat's old inflatable kiddie pool, their iridescent wings shining rainbow colors. But by the second day, keeping a low profile was beginning to get on Nat's nerves, even though he didn't know what else he would have been doing. He was jumpy and irritable, and his mood affected Woody, making him pace up and down the garden restlessly.

"Nat, we need to talk."

Nat rolled his eyes. He'd been sitting in the blow-up pool with a book while Woody dozed fitfully under the apple tree. It was never good when his mum "needed to talk." Usually it was to lecture him for some mistake, or to say that she had found him a "little job to do." Reluctantly he went inside, Woody following at his heels.

His mum was already sitting on the sofa. She looked serious, her hands folded in her lap.

"I'm not deaf, you know," she said gravely, as Nat sat down opposite her.

"What do you mean?" asked Nat, puzzled.

"I keep hearing you talk to Woody," said Jude gently, "like he's a *person*."

"I *don't* talk to him," Nat protested. "Not really. I'm just thinking out loud."

"It's not healthy," said Jude. "It's time you made some real friends: *human* friends."

Nat could feel himself getting annoyed. "Hmmmm," he said, pretending to think hard. "I could call up the Slaughtered Sheep and ask Teddy Davis over for tea, or maybe one of his Neanderthal gang would like to come out with me on Granddad's boat."

"OK," sighed Jude, "point taken. But maybe I didn't mean here in Temple Gurney."

She passed Nat an envelope. Puzzled, he shook out the contents. Two oblong pieces of thin card stock dropped into his hand.

"Two tickets for the Eurostar?" Nat frowned.

"For the train to Paris," said Jude. "Your dad sent them. For you and me."

"But . . . but . . . what about . . . ?" stammered Nat, bewildered.

"Woody will come, too," interrupted Jude hastily. "He won't even need to go into quarantine with the other animals; it's all in Dad's letter."

Nat thought for a moment, his excitement building. "When do we go?"

"Next week," said Jude, hugging him. "Oh, Nat, I've been so worried you wouldn't want to go. This will be a wonderful new start for us."

Nat thought quickly. *It could work.* Now there would be no need for Woody to go with Crescent and the Howlers. True, they would have to stay completely out of sight for a few days longer, but once Woody had crossed the English Channel and set foot in France, the Proteus people would never find him — hopefully.

"Woody will need to be microchipped," said Jude, "and he'll need his own passport."

Nat's face fell. "But that could mean Woody will be weeks behind us."

"Read Dad's letter," urged Jude, "it'll explain everything."

She dropped a kiss on the top of his head, which he rubbed off impatiently, and left him to read the letter. Nat scanned his dad's scrawly, loopy handwriting. If enthusiasm could pay rent and buy groceries, the Carvers would never have had any money troubles at all. Despite his failure to make his fortune as an inventor, no one could accuse Evan Carver of not throwing himself wholeheartedly into a new project. And, as Nat read on, it seemed that for once his dad was actually making more money than he could spend; he was even able to pay his debts.

Nat was so engrossed, he didn't realize that at some stage Woody had left the room. Puzzled, Nat looked out the window, but he couldn't see him anywhere.

Then a muffled noise came from behind the sofa. He froze. He strained his ears; there it was again. He knelt on the cushions and peered over the back. Crouching behind the sofa was a grinning, human-shaped Woody.

"What are you looking so pleased about?" whispered Nat frantically. "You've shifted!"

"It was quick," whispered Woody proudly. "*Smooooooth!* I planned it!"

Nat straightened up. It was bizarre having a conversation with someone who was naked and crouching behind a sofa. *I wonder if I'll ever get used to this,* he thought.

"You will," said Woody.

"*Hey,* you read my mind again," said Nat, forgetting to whisper. What Iona had told them would happen was right: Woody was growing up. His speech was less halting and his vocabulary was improving. If he could control his changes, too, life would be a lot less scary.

"So, you mean, you shifted deliberately?" he asked.

Woody nodded. "Just thought about it, *puuushed* myself, and . . . it worked."

"That," said Nat with satisfaction, "is mega-amazing. Now, can you change back quickly, please, before someone comes in and wonders why there's a weird naked kid behind the sofa?"

"It's all right." Woody grinned. "Apple and Mick are shopping." He cocked his head to one side. "They're in the store with papers of news and lotteries."

"At the supermarket checkout? You can *see* them?" asked Nat, amazed.

"Yup." Woody smiled. "But your mum's in the shower."

Nat's eyes narrowed.

"Oooh *noooo*," said Woody hastily, "I can only hear the water."

"She'll be down soon," whispered Nat. "Before you shift, did you hear what she said?"

"She said you were unhealthy," whispered Woody. "I'm sorry, but I think she meant you needed cyclehatrick help."

"*Psychiatric* help," Nat whispered back. "No, not that. About going to France."

"Yep." Woody beamed, then his face fell. "Not in the car?"

"No, not in the car," agreed Nat. "You've got to travel in a special compartment on the Eurostar train. It goes in a tunnel under the sea between England and France."

Woody looked alarmed. "But . . ."

"Don't worry," said Nat hastily, "it's perfectly safe. And my dad is getting a special license for you, which means you can travel as soon as you've had your vaccinations."

Woody still looked doubtful . . . and *worried*.

"I know." Nat grinned. "It sounds almost too good to be true."

"Maybe it is," said Woody quietly. "I feel funny, like something bad is going to happen."

Nat was alarmed. "What do you mean?"

Woody shrugged. "It's something . . ." He shook his head impatiently. "I dunno, it's beyond me. I can't see it yet."

"Maybe it's nothing," said Nat hopefully. "You've said you sometimes get these feelings and they don't always happen."

Woody smiled, anxious not to spoil Nat's joy at the thought of seeing his father again.

"Now, can you change back, please?" pleaded Nat.

"You want to see?" asked Woody.

Nat hesitated; he felt uncomfortable. As long as it wasn't like the time at the carnival in the parking lot. That had looked horrible—painful, even. He nodded hesitantly.

"Here goes." Woody closed his eyes and crouched low behind the sofa.

As Nat watched, the air surrounding Woody seemed to become visible; it shifted and rippled slightly as the change started. His body seemed to shorten, and his face became oddly elongated as his mouth and nose pushed out to form the wolfish snout. Shimmery white fur sprouted all over his body, and his long tail, fringed with gossamer fur, thrashed to and fro on the living room carpet as though it were a separate being. Then air seemed to drift away again from Woody's body. The transformation had taken just seconds.

"That. Is. So. Cool!" breathed Nat, who could already hear Mick's car pulling up the gravel driveway.

Woody chuffed, a slightly superior expression appearing on his face.

Nat could hear Apple's voice outside the living room door. He glanced back at Woody, and what he saw made him do a double take.

Something about Woody wasn't quite right: *He had two sets of ears.*

"What *are* you doing?" asked Apple incredulously. She stared in disbelief as she entered the living room. Her grandson and his dog were both sitting up straight as boards on the sofa, looking guilty. Strangely, they were both wearing Stetson cowboy hats.

"Those are our line-dancing hats!" stormed Apple, stomping across the room. Nat winced as Apple whipped the hats off and put them back on the shelf. He risked a peek at Woody. *Nooo!* There were still two sets of ears, one furry wolf set and another bald set, which gleamed pinkly human from the sides of his head. Incredibly, Apple hadn't noticed . . . yet.

"Your granddad brought those hats all the way from Texas," she said, annoyed. "I don't want smelly dog fur all over them."

"Sorry, Nan," said Nat, hastily getting up from the sofa. He spun Apple around to face her away from Woody. "Show me some steps."

Apple frowned. "Stop taking the mickey," she scolded. "You hate line dancing."

"No," said Nat earnestly. "I love it. I . . . er . . . I'm thinking of taking it up."

Apple narrowed her eyes. "Well, OK, then, but if you laugh . . ."

While Apple patiently taught Nat her favorite dance, the County Line Cha-Cha, to her favorite song, "Achy Breaky Heart," Woody took his chance and slunk away to hide in the garden.

CHAPTER 15
OUT OF CONTROL

Later, as Nat helped his mum prepare lunch, he, too, felt a growing sense of unease. Despite the good news in his dad's letter, he couldn't help thinking that what Woody had sensed earlier that morning was true: There was something wrong.

When his grandfather burst through the back door brandishing the local paper, Nat was prepared for the worst. He held his breath.

"Look at this," Mick said breathlessly. "Look at the headline."

Nat's insides turned to stone while Mick spread the *North Somerset Reveille* open on the kitchen table. The headline bounced off the page, hitting him like a smack in the face.

DOG RUNS AMOK AT TEMPLE GURNEY SHOW
BY DREW HARDING

The photograph accompanying the story would have made a stunning poster for a horror film—a horror film featuring homicidal wolves. It was Woody, mouth frothing, murderous gleam in his eyes, hurtling across the arena with one thought on his mind: to get Teddy Davis.

"Look at the way the camera caught him," said Mick. "No wonder the Davis kid was frightened!"

Nat said nothing, scanning the story frantically.

The dog, named Woody, was apparently unprovoked and caused damage to many of the exhibits at the fair. One witness told of her terror as the animal ran amok during one of the classes in the dog show. "It was competing in the Dog with the Most Appealing Face category," explained Miss Alice Throgmorton, 57, a judge at the competition. "I'm afraid it didn't have a hope of being placed, even before it started to froth at the mouth."

The dog, thought to be a German shepherd cross, is owned by local man Mick Smith and his family.

*According to well-known local business owner Mr.
Tom Davis, whose son Teddy was attacked, the
dog is a menace and should be muzzled in public.*

Nat couldn't bring himself to read any more. He felt his tan fade to white. This was bad. Worse than bad. He imagined what Crescent would say if she knew about it. *"What part of keeping a low profile didn't you understand?"* she would hiss.

Low profile? Nat thought to himself. *That's a joke.* They might as well have taken out an ad. How long, he wondered, before there'd be a knock at the door? They had to get out.

Apple put her hand on Nat's arm. "No harm done, Nat," she said gently. "Woody didn't actually bite anyone. There's nothing anyone can do about it."

Nat felt near to tears.

"I know," he said, his shoulders slumping. "But the story makes Woody out to be a monster; people will want him to be locked up. . . ."

"Do you mean Teddy Davis?" asked Apple.

Among others, thought Nat with dread.

Mick swallowed hard. "Don't you worry about him," he said. "I'll go and have a word with Tom, try to sort things out."

Nat tried smiling, but his face felt all wrong. "I'm going to take Woody swimming," he said. "Is it all right if we go on the boat, Granddad?"

Mick fetched the key to the *Diamond Lil.* "Don't worry, lad, it'll be fine. There's no real harm in Woody."

Apple watched her grandson and his dog as they walked out of the sunny garden and onto Camellia Lane. Mick picked up the newspaper and studied the photograph of Woody.

"How do you know there's no harm in him?" asked Apple softly.

"Because," said Mick grimly, "if Woody was like the others up at Helleborine Halt, Teddy Davis would be dead by now. Dead, *or worse!*"

Heat radiating upward from the hot pavement gave the deserted lane an eerie, shimmery feel, as though it weren't quite solid. Nat and Woody walked in the shade, deliberately keeping in the shadows. Woody's restlessness had morphed into unease, and he stopped frequently, sniffing the air, his ears back, fur stiff, making Nat as jumpy as a box of frogs. He knew they were vulnerable out in the open like this, and he tried to shake off the horrible feeling that someone was watching them.

At Diamond Beach, bobbing in the small marina, Mick's boat, the *Diamond Lil*, waited quietly by the quay. Once aboard, Nat felt less worried. He gazed out to sea and tried not to think about the consequences of the newspaper story. Woody stood like a figurehead at the prow of the *Diamond Lil*, sniffing the still air and growling low.

"What?" asked Nat, his stomach churning. Woody had fixed his gaze on the rocks above the cove, his body quivering slightly. To Nat's weak human eye, the cliffs seemed deserted. Nat got to his feet and stood next to Woody, shielding his eyes from the sun. It wasn't until he was almost blinded by a flash of silver caught by the brilliant sunshine that he knew Woody's instincts were right.

They were under surveillance.

After some time they could both make out the figures on the cliff. There were three of them, moving closer by the minute. One was definitely Davis. The other two, Nat soon realized, were the slack-jawed Spanner Harris and the pudgy kid who never bathed—Nat didn't know his name. He tried to think.

"We can't go to Iona's," he told a snarling Woody. "We can't risk leading them to Meade Lodge."

Woody now wore the same murderous expression he had in the newspaper photograph. Saliva dripped from his mouth; his hackles were stiff. Nat glanced wildly around. The *Diamond Lil* was blocked in by three other boats in the marina. It would take him ages to steer it out. Davis and his cronies were still a way up on the cliffs. It would take time for them to climb down to the beach. "C'mon!" Nat shouted to Woody. "We'll have to make a run for it!"

Woody jumped up first, with Nat following. He led Nat away from Teddy Davis. A faint shout went up: Davis had spotted them. Woody still led the way, racing for a rocky inlet, which Nat hoped would give them a good place to hide.

Thinking and running is not an easy combination, but whether it was adrenaline or a growing feeling of outrage,

Nat felt his anger take over and fear slip away. He was more than angry. He was absolutely furious. Davis was frightened to death of Woody; surely he wouldn't want to come within biting distance? He was mental, but he wasn't stupid. Nat stopped and waited, legs trembling slightly with anticipation. Woody came galloping back.

"We'll face them," Nat panted. "But don't bite anyone, OK? Just do the eye thing, that'll be enough."

Near the top of the cliff, Teddy Davis gripped his BB gun tightly. He'd wanted to take Carver on his own, separate him from that stupid mongrel and frighten the little runt to death. He gestured to Spanner Harris to move farther down so they could get a better look at Carver and the dog. The plan had been to stay higher than them, to be able to get a clear shot at the mutt—just to scare it, of course. Teddy debated whether to follow and risk being attacked. But he had his gun, didn't he? Any weirdness and he'd threaten to use it.

Fueled by adrenaline and hate, Teddy Davis followed Spanner Harris down the path after Nat Carver. Twenty minutes later, Davis and his gang of two stopped about twenty feet away from their quarry. And by then Nat's fury had been replaced by a feeling like being kicked in the stomach.

Teddy Davis had a *gun*.

There was a ten-second face-off, but to all of them the seconds seemed like hours. It was Nat who broke the unbearable silence.

"So what are you going to do now, *Tiger*, shoot us?" said Nat, surprised his voice sounded normal.

But something weird was happening to the older boy. His eyes appeared glazed, as though he were thinking of something else. Then he grinned maniacally. He raised the BB gun up to his shoulder and took aim.

A noise like a shouting mosquito flew past Nat's left ear. *Peeooow!*

A small chunk of quartz popped out of the rock next to Woody.

Nat stared at it in disbelief. "Go!" he shouted at Woody. They took off like Olympic athletes out of the starter blocks.

"Get them!" Davis howled in fury.

Nat and Woody clambered across the rocks, heading for the ridge across one of the channels of water. Too late,

Nat realized his mistake. Massive rocks rose above them; there was no way out of the bay. They were trapped.

Peeeeooow! This time, the pellet struck Woody in the chest. He yipped in surprise and pain. Nat gasped in horror and looked around. He could hear Teddy's crazed laughter.

Pudgy Badger O'Neil also glanced at Teddy Davis uneasily. He was shocked. He hadn't bargained for anything like this; Teddy looked demented. Badger watched with growing unease as Davis loaded five more pellets into the magazine and aimed at the dog again. He could see its eyes burning like fire, and it was standing in front of the Carver kid as though it was shielding him from the pellets. Teddy started shooting again, always aiming for the animal in the chest, where the white fur was stained with brilliant red blood. Everyone else seemed frozen in horror, unable to move.

Then a red light popped on inside Badger O'Neil's brain.

Oh, this ain't right! he thought in dismay. Tiger Davis had gone too far this time, and Badger, who already had a juvenile record, had no wish to be caught up in this kind of thing.

"I'm out of here," he told the other two curtly. "You might wanna have a word with yourself, dude," he added to Teddy. "You're totally out of control."

Badger's departure seemed to bring Teddy to his senses. His eyes cleared and were no longer, as Spanner Harris said later, "kind of empty, like."

Teddy Davis slowly put down the BB gun, looking at it as though he were surprised to see it there.

For a few moments, Spanner gazed at Teddy in dismay, as if he had never seen him before in his life. *Oh, this was off-the-charts baaaad,* Spanner was thinking. *Teddy fired his rifle at a dog!*

"What're you looking at?" growled Teddy. "Come on, we'll go home an' I'll kill you at pool."

CHAPTER 16
THE LADY VANISHES

Nat was frantic. He didn't even notice Teddy Davis and Spanner Harris leave. He was up to his elbows in sticky blood and fur, desperately trying to pry the pellets out of poor Woody's chest.

"I can't get any more out," he fretted, shaking his head in defeat. "If we leave them in, you'll get lead poisoning!"

Woody sat up straight and, to Nat's distress, started to rake himself with his powerful claws. As he scratched, blood splashed copiously onto the rocks below, and the pellets Nat had not been able to reach plopped out in a gooey mess. He had another, much more pleasant, shock a few seconds later when he inspected Woody's wounds.

"They've nearly healed already!" Nat exclaimed. "If you weren't covered in blood, it would be as though the pellets had never been there."

Woody flashed Nat a look as if to say, *No biggie. Me, I get shot full of lead all the time.* He shook himself and, as though waiting for Nat to get a grip, stood expectantly. He badly needed Iona and the sanctuary of Meade Lodge.

Nat was confident that Teddy Davis had gone — from the weird look on his face, he'd thought Davis was going to puke. As he and Woody made their way to East Valley, Nat was still in shock, but he was also very aware of how strange they both must look, stained maroon with Woody's blood. He hoped they wouldn't see too many people.

The reached Meade Lodge in a daze, without meeting anyone on the way. But when they got to the house, it possessed none of the sunlit splendor they'd seen just a couple of days ago. Sheltered from the morning sun, the mullioned windows seemed to gleam with crafty malevolence, as if someone unseen were watching them from within.

Nat stared in dismay at the sight that greeted them. The gates were ajar and badly charred; it looked like someone had set fire to them to force entry. The garden was deserted and still, all the life drawn out of it. As they approached the little herb garden at the back of the house, they saw the kitchen door hanging off-kilter from one hinge.

"*Oh, no*, look!" cried Nat, his knees wobbling. On closer inspection, the door appeared to have been *ripped* off: Deep grooves ran through the ancient wood, as though someone with a knife, or maybe—and Nat didn't dwell on this—something with long claws, had raked it. Nat was comforted by Woody's body language, his cocked ears and tail carried like a banner confirming his feeling that whatever *had* been here had gone. *But where was Iona?* Woody's claws clicked on the stone floor as he led them through the ruined kitchen door and into the banquet hall.

There were no delicious spicy smells, no trace of the excitement they had felt on their first visit. Iona was the heart and soul of the house, and without her presence they might as well have been in a mausoleum.

"It's so cold in here," said Nat, shivering. "It's like the house has died."

Then a noise interrupted the silence: A soul-shriveling shrieking came from above. Woody shot past Nat like a heat-seeking missile, leaping up the entire staircase in two bounds. Nat followed, the noise getting gradually louder as he climbed the stairs. Then it stopped. Wildly, Nat looked around. All the doors were closed except one. He ran to the end of the corridor, just in time to see Woody's tail disappear inside.

"Wait!" Nat called, and bounded after Woody. The shrieking noise started up again; it sounded like someone was slowly feeding a cat through one of those mangles that used to squeeze the water out of clothes.

All Nat could see when he entered the elegant bedroom was Woody's furry white back end sticking out from under a vast, four-poster bed. His long tail was slowly wagging to and fro, and whatever was making this unholy racket appeared to be under the bed. Nat knelt down and counted to five before he reluctantly pushed his face under the frilly bottom of the bedspread.

Two familiar lapis lazuli eyes glared back at him.

"Clawdia!" He laughed, shaky with relief. He grasped her front legs and pulled her out as gently as he could. She hissed at Woody, but seemed happy enough to snuggle into Nat's arms, still fizzing like a dying firework.

"I wish you could tell us what happened to your mistress," murmured Nat, stroking her delicate head.

Clawdia yowled dolefully and Woody whined miserably.

"I can't believe it," Nat spluttered, near hysteria. "I'm stuck in the weirdest situation of my life, and neither of you creatures can talk!"

This thought sent him off into wild laughter, but he pulled himself together when he felt Woody's breath on his face. Nat felt bad. Obviously his friend still couldn't change whenever he wanted to, despite all the practice. It wasn't fair to complain.

"Sorry," he said gruffly, wiping his eyes on the lacy bedspread. "C'mon. Let's go and . . ." He stopped talking abruptly.

Woody was staring at him, fixing him with a topaz glare just like the one Nat had seen way back in Tate's yard.

Uh-oh, thought Nat. The evening sunlight seemed to be sucked out of the bedroom, leaving a shimmery, dream-like glow. He steeled himself as he felt again the strange sensation of Woody pushing at his mind. *But what? What was he trying to show him? Would it be something that had already happened? Something that was going to happen? What?* The glow faded, just as the sun had seemed to go out in Tate's yard, and Nat tried in vain to see. *Please don't let it be anything too horrible*, he prayed.

Nat's senses were overwhelmed by a hissing, spitting sound. His eyes widened as a flash streaked up Iona's grand staircase as though the hounds of hell were following. *Clawdia!* Seconds later, Nat gasped in horror: Someone, or something, was after her.

A large, mottled paw grasped the ornate rail of Iona's grand staircase. Just before the image faded, Nat saw the owner of the paw. It was the face of his nightmares: *Lucas Scale.*

"Uh?" The vision had gone. "That was telepathy, right?" said Nat shakily. "Lucas Scale was here, wasn't he?"

Woody yipped and swiped the door with his paws, anxious to keep moving.

"Iona might have left us a clue," said Nat urgently. "You take downstairs and I'll take this floor."

Between them, they searched every inch of Meade Lodge. There were thirteen bedrooms to check, two with bathrooms en suite, and a massive chamberlike room with a sunken bath in the center of the floor. As far as Nat could see, there were no signs of disturbance. If Iona didn't come back, they would have to make some permanent arrangements for Clawdia, but Nat erased that thought from his mind. He didn't like to think of Iona not coming back. It sounded so final. As though she were dead.

Leaving Clawdia to her refuge under the bed, Nat ran downstairs in search of Woody, but there was no sign of him. *Where is he?* he thought to himself, beginning to panic. When he reached the bottom step, he wondered whether to call out for Woody. The silence was unnerving, but he didn't want to break it, just in case there was still something lurking in the shadows.

He entered the banquet hall. The rows of computers sat there, staring at him with their blank, silent screens. Nat shivered.

Get a grip, he told himself sternly. *Get a grip, get Woody, and get out.* Then a sudden movement to his left made him freeze.

A book lay open on Iona's table. Nat instantly felt certain it had been left for him. *Maybe Iona left it as a clue.* Its pages fluttered in a breeze from nowhere, making a nasty, papery hiss. Nat found himself moving, almost drifting, toward it. *Like in my nightmares,* he thought, his throat dry. As he drew closer, the book snapped shut with a loud *smack!* Nat almost screamed out loud. He forced himself to read the title. Written in bold black letters were the words *Nightmares: A Compendium*.

Nat swallowed hard and reached a shaky hand out toward the cover. Before he could touch it, the book sprang open again, almost knocking him over. The pages riffled and fanned themselves fussily, opening at last to a picture of a boy and a large white wolf, which looked uncannily like himself and Woody. To Nat's delight, the picture began to move and the sketch turned into a living but tiny version of boy and Wolven. Nat breathed in the sea air and the salty, eggy smell of the seaweed as he pushed his face closer to the page. He heard himself laugh as his tiny self and Woody ran down to the shoreline. It looked as though it was a late summer's evening. Nat watched in delight as the pair played in the surf.

Abruptly, the scene changed to a leafy, wooded glade. His delight turned to dismay as dark clouds rolled inland toward the woods, where the boy and Wolven were now enjoying a walk. Then Nat spotted a third figure, in the corner of the page. It appeared to be watching them.

Nat strained to see the tall, thin figure more clearly, and then wished he hadn't. The watcher turned away from the pair in the woods and looked straight at Nat. Terrified, Nat tried to look away from the burning orange eyes. "*No,*" he whispered, but he couldn't break his gaze.

The figure grew larger on the page, as if a camera were zooming in on it. Nat felt himself being drawn closer in. The man grinned at Nat, showing enormous teeth; the smell of its breath made him gag. Nat saw now that it wasn't a man at all. It was some kind of werewolf. The same horrible, mottled, gray-skinned thing he had seen in his nightmares: *Lucas Scale!* Never mind being politically correct; the thing grinning at him from the page was a crazed werewolf. He tried to tear his terrified gaze away from the loathsome mottled wolf thing. It raised a misshapen paw in a kind of mocking salute. Nat couldn't help himself. He screamed.

A large white furry object hurtled out of nowhere and knocked him away from the evil book. As Nat fell onto the stone floor, he saw that Woody had grasped the book in his jaws. He let it drop to the floor and began pummeling it with his paws, gripping random pages with his teeth and shredding them to a pulp. Pages flew everywhere, swooping around the room like white birds. When *Nightmares: A Compendium* had been mashed beyond recognition and the pages lay strewn around as though they were dead at last, Woody threw himself on Nat, chuffing and yipping, trying to console him.

"OK, OK!" Nat laughed shakily. "I'll be fine once I've had cyclehatrick help."

Woody wagged his tail and pulled at Nat's jeans with his teeth.

"Absolutely," agreed Nat. "Let's get out of here!"

But Woody raced off in the opposite direction. When Nat caught up with him, he found him staring intently at the arched doorway to the basement.

"Come on, let's get out of here," repeated Nat. But Woody wouldn't budge.

"What now . . . ?" asked Nat wearily. He walked over to the door, squinting to see what had interested Woody so much. What he saw made his heart heavy.

In the soft lime plaster surrounding the arch, almost invisible to the human eye, were some faint scratches and grooves. Stuck in one of the deeper grooves was a tiny fragment of what looked like a torn-off fingernail. Nat pried it out and held it in the palm of his hand.

"I guess you were right," he told Woody sadly.

The fingernail had belonged to a person who had tried to hang on with all her might, to stop herself from being taken away by a monster. It belonged to a person who painted her nails jade green, to match her eyes. Scale had taken Iona!

CHAPTER 17
TIGER IN THE BAG!

Teddy Davis and Spanner Harris walked in silence toward Temple Cross. Teddy's mouth felt dry; his heart was hammering. He felt like he was going to be sick. This was a whole lot more serious than thieving the Christmas Club money from the staff at the Slaughtered Sheep. (He hadn't been able to sit down for a week when his old man discovered it was him who had nicked it.) It was even worse than setting the clawed traps, although luckily he had never been caught for that. Except by Mick Smith. Teddy supposed he should be grateful the old hippie hadn't told his dad.

How had he let things get so badly out of hand? After the excitement of hunting down Carver and his homicidal mutt, he was slowly beginning to realize what had happened: He had actually *shot* at something with his BB gun, actually *shot* that dumb mutt of Carver's. If his dad found out, he would go absolutely crazy. Teddy would be grounded for the rest of his *life*, let alone summer vacation, and he'd lose the air rifle for sure. He had been told that *under no circumstances* was he *ever* to use it to shoot anything but rats. The mutt had bled everywhere. Carver would be bound to tell.

He'd only been showing off, and yeah, he liked to use his fists now and then, but what had possessed him to actually shoot? A thought struck him then. It *had* been as though he were possessed. Like something had been gnawing away at him, nagging him to pick up the rifle and take a shot at Carver. Badger had been right: It was like . . . well, like he had no control.

"Bye then, Tiger," said Spanner Harris unhappily, sensing correctly there was to be no game of pool. "See yuz tommorer?"

"Yeah," said Teddy, trying to sound normal. He watched as Spanner's broad back disappeared around the corner. Teddy found himself alone, by the edge of the great East Wood.

I'll deny it all, thought Teddy wildly. He'd throw the gun away, and no one would ever know. Yeah, it would be his word against Carver's, and without the gun there would be no proof! Spanner and Badger would do as he told them. But that mutt . . . it had been bleeding quite bad. For once, Teddy felt a shiver of conscience. He needed a place to hide the air rifle, somewhere it would never be found.

The sun seemed to lose its warmth, and he shivered again. Teddy and his buddies usually avoided the woods like they avoided school, but it would be an ideal place to bury the gun. He continued along the dusty track, having decided that the picnic area was the least spooky place to approach the woods. As he entered the clearing, he was surprised to see an enormous, black, four-wheel-drive vehicle with tinted windows parked there. It was the kind of cool monster wagon you could only import from America. Despite his morbid mood, Teddy couldn't help but admire it. He found himself moving toward it to get a better look.

The SUV hummed slightly; maybe the engine was cooling. Violet blue lights flashed rhythmically, pulsating along with the soft noise the engine made, calming Teddy's mood. It was nice watching the lights; all his worries were fading away. *Nah*, it'd be OK about Nat Carver and the gun. He would chuck it in the sea and that would be the end of it. Why had he been so worked up about that stupid little runt anyway? Teddy grinned vacantly, all the while watching the lights intently.

A movement made him glance across to the picnic area for a moment. All the breath left Teddy's lungs. For there, sitting at one of the tables, eating a sandwich from a vast wicker picnic basket, was the most hideous apparition Teddy had ever seen, even in his most graphic nightmares.

The creature stood up slowly. It was tall and thin, its facial features arranged halfway between a man and a wolf. The parts of its body not covered by clothing were the color of dead flesh, mottled different shades of gray and green, and covered in a sparse, black fuzz of hair. It was dressed in a T-shirt with an iron-on transfer of Ozzy Osbourne on the front, and a pair of too big, faded jeans. It grinned at Teddy, showing a snaggled arrangement of impossible teeth. If it was trying for friendly, the effect was just the opposite. Teddy found himself unable to run away—it was as though his legs had frozen. His throat was affected similarly. He couldn't even scream.

"Good afternoon, young man," said the wolf thing chummily. "Fancy a sandwich?"

Teddy just stood there, his mouth opening and shutting like a stranded goldfish.

"I'll take that as a no," purred the wolf thing. "Come and take the weight off your feet. You look tired."

Teddy suddenly *did* feel tired; he could have slept for a week. He rubbed his stinging eyes with the hem of his T-shirt.

Somehow, the wolf thing had got up from the table and was standing in front of him, without Teddy even noticing it had moved. *How was this happening?* It must be the shock of shooting that dog and feeling guilty about what he'd done to Nat Carver. This couldn't be real.

But *ugh* . . . The wolf thing smelled very, very bad. It reminded Teddy of rotten fish. The wolf had amazing eyes, though. He could look at them forever. . . .

When the wolf thing bit him, he felt nothing.

Lucas Scale howled in triumph. This tall, stocky fellow would make a fine werewolf. He had all the potential needed for their indestructible army: malice, strength, and greed. He flung the boy into a burlap sack and tossed the remains of the picnic basket aside. Although the boy was tall, Scale swung the sack over his shoulder with ease, the unconscious body thudding dully as Scale threw him unceremoniously into the back of the black Hummer.

Lucas Scale howled along to "Born to Be Wild" as he drove the monster car expertly through the narrow roads toward Helleborine Halt. His black, wormy heart was further lifted by the promise of capturing the Wolven.

Your turn next. He grinned at the thought. *Oh, yes! You and your little human friend! What fun we will have.*

CHAPTER 18

THE CHAMBER OF THE WOLF

The doors of the elevator slid together with a gentle *whooooosh*. Two massive figures, identically dressed in immaculate Valentino designer suits, faced each other in uneasy silence as they descended deep into the bowels of Helleborine Halt. They were late for an emergency meeting. Dr. Gruber's mood had been precarious all week, and neither of them was keen on watching one of Gruber's full-blown tantrums.

"You ready for this, bro?" inquired Vincent Spaghetti.

Angelo Spaghetti nodded. "Ready as I'll ever be, dude."

The doors opened and the Spaghetti twins stepped out, their black patent Prada shoes twinkling in the subdued lighting that lined the winding corridors of rock. Angelo shuddered at the cries coming from one of the holding cells in the cavern below.

"Sounds like there's a new kid on the block," Vincent said morosely.

"The new blood," agreed Angelo, and shivered. *Poor, cursed creature,* he thought to himself.

Angelo hated it beneath the Halt. If evil was contagious, as Angelo believed it to be, then the Halt was riddled with it. He remembered the pride in Lucas Scale's voice when he had first shown them what lay beneath the grand old house. He had taken them down the same dimly lit stairwell they walked in now, leading them to a secure unit, aptly named the Chamber of the Wolf, where the project's first lycanthrope had been housed in the 1960s.

Scale had provided Angelo and Vincent with a history of the Halt; a kind of lesson in evil. He said the building had been exposed to centuries of wickedness, all adding to the atmosphere of violent malevolence.

"The Halt was commissioned by Sir Henry Horwood in the early eighteenth century," Scale had droned. "The site was deliberately chosen because of the Paleolithic caves inside the hill. Sir Henry's architect was able to join the house to the caves."

"Sounds like he had a lot to hide," remarked Angelo.

Scale grinned, showing all his snaggly teeth. "Indeed. A devil worshipper of some notoriety, I believe."

"Sounds like a real prince," snarled Vincent.

Scale ignored him. "The architect found that the caves were littered with dismembered skeletons." He chuckled. "Apparently the early cave dwellers had been cannibals."

"Nice." Angelo winced.

The twins had also learned that staff numbers at the Halt were at an all-time low, due to many of the original staff having been eaten. Some of the "residents" — creatures that had been studied in the first project — had successfully replaced them. This suited Gabriel Gruber, because he didn't have to pay them, keeping him well within his governmental budget.

The Home Office, which was the government office in charge of Proteus, left the running of the project to Gabriel Gruber now that Paxton was out of the picture. World events of the past few years had dictated a need for the type of monster that Gabriel was trying to create. Certain sections of the British government wholeheartedly agreed that Indestructible Warriors were the way forward, and they weren't too worried about how it happened, as long as nobody could blame it on them.

The twins reached their destination and removed their polarized sunglasses, revealing eyes the color of molten lava. "Here we go, bro," said Vincent. "Whatever he says, just agree with him."

Angelo nodded nervously. Although he was a werewolf, and built like a Sherman tank, he was so scared of Gabriel Gruber that he had trouble concentrating whenever he was in the same room. Vincent waved his magnetic pass at the door. It opened silently, revealing two people already settled around the table. Gabriel beamed at them expansively, his handsome face hectic with glee.

"Gentlemen," Gabriel Gruber proclaimed with a nod, "better late than never."

Scale sat on Gruber's right, a smirk hanging off his raddled face.

Vincent lifted his lip in a snarl as he took his seat by Scale. How he hated him. The brothers had been reluctant converts to lycanthropy, and still detested Lucas Scale for being responsible. Five years ago, just one bite of Scale's jagged, blackened teeth had converted them both into werewolves and changed their lives forever. However, because they were experts at controlling their changes and far classier than most of the other werewolves in the Halt, they were personal favorites of Gabriel Gruber's, and had quickly become his bodyguards.

An air of expectancy throbbed in the chilly, air-conditioned room.

"I know you will appreciate it if I come straight to the point." Gabriel beamed. "Contrary to the expectations of our doubting friends at the Whitehall Home Office in London, we have achieved our goal. We have the Wolven."

Angelo and Vincent joined in with the usual cheers and pats on the back that they knew were expected of them.

Gabriel held up his hands to quell the applause.

"I am afraid none of you can take any credit," he said, his smile now ancient history, "because, of course, although I am pleased, HE SHOULD HAVE BEEN FOUND MONTHS AGO."

Even Lucas Scale sat up straight, the smirk wiped from his face.

Vincent hid a grin and nudged his twin. *Oh, boy*, he thought, *here we go again*.

They watched in mute embarrassment as Gabriel Gruber stood up and expressed his displeasure through the medium of dance. Face flushed, he pranced around the room, quivering with temper, knocking files from the shelves in fury. He swept the espresso machine off the glass table, pausing only long enough to watch as it smashed into expensive smithereens. Gabriel's tantrum gained momentum as he pirouetted over to Lucas Scale and thrashed him soundly with a rolled-up copy of the day's *North Somerset Reveille* newspaper. Eventually he stopped and got his breath back, then carried on ranting.

"The pathetic attempts of my colleague here, with his supposedly 'enhanced awareness,' failed miserably. IF I HADN'T READ THIS BLASTED LOCAL RAG, I WOULDN'T BE ANY THE WISER!"

The three still sitting at the round table bowed their heads like chastened schoolchildren. Gabriel Gruber was right; if the Wolven *had* been in Temple Gurney all this time, he had successfully outwitted them all. Lucas Scale had even dragged Lady Iona to Helleborine Halt for interrogation, but in the two days he'd been questioning her she had denied any knowledge of the whereabouts of the Wolven.

"You said you had the Wolven," said Vincent bravely. "So where is he?"

Gabriel flashed his perfect white teeth.

"We take him this evening," he said. "There were one or two little details that needed to be taken care of first." He glanced at Scale, who nodded.

"Lucas here has created a little mess in the deer park and pinned it on our Wolven friend. I'm afraid the local police force has been alerted, but of course, we have more power than them."

"Why can't we go now?" asked Scale, keen to get his paws on the prize.

"Because," said Gruber curtly, impatience making a knobbly rope of vein throb at his temple, "this way, we take back what is ours, legally, with no fuss, and more important, with no violence. Nothing that can be traced back to Proteus."

"But what if the boy, Nathaniel Carver, has removed him?" Angelo asked quickly.

Gabriel's noble brow creased slightly. "Don't you worry your furry head about that," he drawled condescendingly. "Nat Carver is a little boy. He has no idea about the Wolven's powers. I don't think we need to trouble ourselves about him."

"But Angelo's right," protested Vincent. "The boy could—"

"We are merely taking back what is ours," interrupted Gabriel sharply. "Trust me. It'll be like taking candy from a baby."

CHAPTER 19
ONE FOR SORROW . . .

"Right! Ready? Go!" shouted Nat.

Woody, his eyes tightly shut in concentration, fur quivering stiffly, *puuuushed* with all his being. Nat held his breath as the outline of Woody's body blurred in the strong sunlight, the lines rippling as though underwater. Seconds later, Woody stood before him in human form, his bare chest maroon with dried blood.

"Come on." Nat grinned. "Time to go home and intro—"

There was a soft rushing noise, like air being sucked out of a container. Nat stared in horror. There was something terribly wrong: Woody was disappearing! His facial features looked as though they were made of wax; it was as if he were collapsing into himself.

"Woody!" Nat panicked. "What's happening to you?"

Woody's body morphed into a long, thin shape; maybe

it was trying to halt the collapse by stretching itself. Nat watched helplessly until the molecules of air became visible again, pushing Woody's body back into Wolven form.

"Thank goodness!" cried Nat, trembling in relief. "I don't know what happened then, but I thought you were a goner!"

Woody stood still, his topaz eyes blinking in the sunlight.

"Never mind," said Nat, still shaken. "I was hoping if you came back with me in human form it would prove our story. We're going to have to go back home, and I'm going to have to rely on you to show me if anything, *anything at all*, is wrong."

Woody stared right back at him, ears pricked, tail held high: the body language of an alpha wolf.

"I'll take that as a yes." Nat grinned again. "I'm going to tell them everything. They won't believe me, but we've got no choice."

The one big thing that Nat didn't even want to admit to himself was that it was a 99.999 percent certainty that someone from Proteus had seen, or been told about, the newspaper story.

But everything at Camellia Lane looked exactly as it had when they'd left that morning. If it hadn't been for Woody's blood-caked fur, Nat could almost imagine that the shooting and the visit to Meade Lodge had never happened. The only vehicles Nat could see outside number eleven were his mum's old clunker and Mick's red Mini Cooper.

In the kitchen his family was sitting at the table, their expressions as grave as those of funeral mourners.

"Have you got something to tell us?" asked Mick, his knees popping as he rose from the table. Nat had never seen his granddad look so grim before. It was like looking at a stranger.

Nat opened his mouth to speak, a torrent of words lining up to fall out. There was so much he wanted to say, but his tongue remained stubbornly superglued to the roof of his mouth.

"The police are on their way over," continued Mick, his lips set in a grim line. "I just got off the phone with Bill Beechgood."

"*Sergeant* Beechgood?" asked Nat, finding his tongue. "Why?"

Mick's tone softened. "I'm sorry, son," he said, "but they're coming to take Woody away."

The police! This wasn't what Nat had expected to hear at all.

"The sergeant's acting on a report from Tom Davis, Teddy Davis's father," said Mick. "A number of his deer have been killed."

"Not just killed, Nat," said Jude quietly. *"Annihilated."*

"But wha . . . ," started Nat. Then a cold fear stole over him. "They think it's Woody? But he's a vegetarian."

Mick shook his bald head impatiently, making his earrings dance.

"This is no time for jokes," he said grimly. "Someone reported a large white dog running from the deer park with blood all over its chest and muzzle. I don't have to be a bloomin' brain surgeon to figure out they were describing Woody."

"Woody *has* got blood all over him," said Nat, relieved. "But Teddy Davis did it. He fired a BB gun at us."

Mick's eyes narrowed slightly. "*What?* And you didn't think to tell us about something as serious as this?"

Nat swallowed. "It only just happened. I was going to tell you as soon as I . . ."

Mick interrupted him. "Where's Woody now?" he demanded.

Nat pointed to the garden, trembling. Mick marched Nat over to the kitchen window.

"There. What's that on his chest?"

"But that's his *own* blood. I told you . . ." Nat paled beneath his tan. "Do you all really think Woody is a killer?"

Mick pursed his lips. "I wouldn't have thought so a couple of days back," he admitted, "but you must admit, he's been acting funny lately."

He threw the paper in front of Nat, and the photo of Woody glared up at him from the *North Somerset Reveille*.

"You laughed about that this morning," said Nat bitterly.

Mick narrowed his eyes. "That was before this business with Tom Davis's deer," he said.

Nat held out his blood-streaked hands. "This is Woody's blood," he said. "I tried to get the pellets out."

Mick frowned and marched outside. Two minutes later, he came back into the kitchen, his face white with anger.

"I don't blame you for trying to save Woody," he said. "But telling lies isn't going to help, Nat. There are no injuries to that dog's chest."

"Yes, that's right," said Nat, his face flushed. "The wounds have healed already."

Everyone looked at Nat in bewilderment.

"I need to tell you something about Woody," he said breathlessly. "He's not a dog at all, he's a Wolven: a supernatural being who can change shape."

Mick stared at his grandson, shaking his head. "A *what*? No, he can't be . . . he's not like . . ."

"That's *enough*," interrupted Jude. "Even if you're telling the truth about the deer, why make up stories? What's *wrong* with you?"

But Nat was staring at Apple. There was something in her eyes. Something like *belief*?

"Nan?" implored Nat. "You believe me, don't you? The tattoo . . . it all makes sense. Woody was part of an experiment to create a new breed of shape-shifting fighting machines—"

"Stop." Jude's face was white. "Just stop this crazy talk *now*." Nat had never seen his mum so upset.

"Oh, forget it," he said, near to tears, and ran out of the kitchen.

He didn't waste a second. He raced upstairs, put a few things into his battered rucksack, tiptoed down to the living room, and sneaked out the French doors.

Just minutes later, two policemen, one of them Bill Beechgood, arrived at the front door. Grim-faced, Mick let them in.

"You know why we're here, Mick?" asked Sergeant Beechgood, removing his helmet.

Mick nodded. "Bill, it could still be a case of mistaken identity."

"I'm sorry, sir," said the younger policeman. "We have to take the dog away."

"Nat has told us he's innocent," protested Jude. "I was dubious at first, but Woody is the gentlest dog. . . ."

"Come on now, Jude," chided Sergeant Beechgood. "You've only got to look at this week's *Reveille* to know that's not strictly true. If he's innocent like you say, there are tests that can be done to prove it either way."

Something large and black pulled up outside 11 Camellia Lane. It blocked out the evening sunshine from the kitchen, spraying gravel all over Apple's luminous green lawn. It was, thought Apple as she looked out the window, the type of black monstrosity driven solely by government officials.

A strange hush came over the gathering in Apple's homey kitchen. The feeling of anticipation was not a good one, for this unnatural quietness was accompanied by a shiver of fear, verging on terror. Instinctively, they all moved closer to each other, all except Apple, who waited in the hall, listening grimly for the inevitable knock.

When Apple opened the door, she tried not to flinch in shock. The strange visitor made her blood curdle into chilly pools in her veins. He was dressed bizarrely, in a very chic suit, its knife-edge creases accentuating his muscular, slightly bowed legs. His eyes were hidden by dark glasses and, despite the heat, he wore a white scarf and a trilby hat.

Two enormous, identical fellows, also wearing sunglasses, flanked the monstrous car as if waiting for instructions. Scale pushed rudely past Apple into the kitchen.

"Ah, I see we have the company of our most excellent police force," he said, his voice muffled slightly by his scarf. "I am instructed by Her Majesty's government to relieve them of the task. I have come for the perpetrator of this most dreadful crime against your most beautiful wildlife." He drew himself up theatrically. "Yes, you see, I have come to take the wolf away."

Jude bravely stepped forward; she had never seen anyone quite so strange in her life. "Woody's no wolf, and there's no proof he's guilty of killing the deer."

Scale didn't even bother to look at her, but his hidden, busy eyes flickered around the kitchen, searching for his prize.

"Madam, I beg to differ. The animal is a hybrid wolf, bred at the Proteus Institute and stolen from our premises by a drinking partner of your father's."

Jude's eyes widened at the reference to Proteus. *The tattoo!* Suddenly, she felt very sick and afraid. *Nat had been telling the truth!*

Sergeant Beechgood, trying to be as brave as Jude, stepped forward indignantly.

"Oi, mate, we got here first," he blustered. "We've been instructed to remove the dog and take it down to the station."

Scale ignored him. "It is one of the most dangerous animals in the world. We have come to take it back to the controlled conditions of the Institute."

Mick suddenly snapped back to life. The appearance of this strange government official at this exact moment seemed very suspicious to him, and he'd rather believe Nat than this creep any day.

"My grandson has explained to me why Woody has blood on him, and I believe him," he said bluntly. "This is a frame-up."

"And I'll allow the police to take Woody," said Apple calmly, "but not you. The claims you are making are preposterous."

Scale signaled to the two figures flanking the black vehicle. Immediately, Angelo and Vincent Spaghetti swooped down the drive, springing catlike through the kitchen door. Vincent held a muzzle and a heavy chain in his gloved hands; Angelo wielded a stick that looked like an electric cattle prod, the ones slaughterers use in an abattoir. They stood, their bodies taking up most of the kitchen, apparently awaiting further instructions from their vile master.

"Search the grounds," Scale ordered.

Mick stepped forward. "There's no need for this," he said, pressing his face as close as he could bear to Scale's. "I won't have my grandson upset. Don't you dare take another step without a warrant."

Through the lenses of his dark glasses, Scale's eyes flashed. "I think you will find my authority overrides any warrant," he said, producing a piece of paper. He thrust it roughly at Sergeant Beechgood, who studied the document intently. After a few seconds, Bill Beechgood looked up. Apple knew by the expression on his face that the news was not good.

"I'm really sorry, Mick, but seems he's right," he said with regret. "This . . . er . . . gentleman has the right to remove the animal under the Dangerous Wild Animals Act of 1976."

Apple shook her head. Whatever Woody was, he was not a killer. Of this she was certain. Scale made a noise in the back of his throat that sounded like a strangled howl of triumph, and nodded to the two suits. There was a scuffle as Mick tried to stop them from gaining access to the back garden, but they were much bigger than him; he didn't stand a chance.

Scale followed his heavies into the garden. It was deserted. Apple's hammock swung in the gentle breeze, the table and chairs set for a late barbecue Mick had planned. No Woody, no Nat.

"WHERE ARE THEY?" Scale screamed. Everyone except the two suits shrank back, shocked. Scale paced up and down Apple's garden, apoplectic with rage, kicking the outdoor furniture and shouting instructions to his two besuited accomplices. Sergeant Beechgood and his young companion watched in disbelief.

Apple and Jude exchanged nervous glances. Indeed, where were they?

Scale ordered the house to be searched. When it proved to be as empty as the garden, Scale whirled to face Apple, who was watching calmly.

"You!" He pushed his face close to hers. "Where have you hidden them?"

Apple smiled. "It's time you got what you came for. I think you will find it in the shed."

Scale glanced at Apple uncertainly. He knew they had already searched the shed, which was filled with human junk: old bicycles, congealed paint, and other such rubbish. This fat woman was playing with him, but at this point he had nothing to lose.

The shed barely stood; it had been in the garden since Jude was a little girl. Scale's pawlike hand shook slightly as he turned the knob. He pulled the rickety door toward him.

Jude and Mick held their breath. Apple stood quietly, a beatific smile on her face.

The noise was sudden and massive. From the small confines of the shed, there appeared hundreds of black-and-white birds, their black feathers shining iridescent blue and turquoise in the afternoon sunlight. Their wings beat a tattoo, sounding like millions of gloved hands clapping, their *chaw chaw chaw* cries adding to the cacophony as they attacked Scale. The birds swooped, claws outstretched, beaks open. Already, they had knocked his trilby to the ground and his pointed ears were bloody with peck marks, but his sunglasses still protected his eyes. One bird, attracted by the glint of the silver frame, swooped down and swiped the dark glasses from Scale's muzzle, revealing eyes the color of molten lava. He scrabbled on the luminous grass, useless feet slipping on the luxuriant turf.

Angelo and Vincent Spaghetti had retreated for the cover of the Hummer. Being covered in bird poo was not in their job description. Fearful for his eyes, Scale screamed for mercy, his scarf unraveling to reveal his dreadful face. There was little humanity left in the creature writhing on Apple's bright green lawn.

"Call them off, witch!" he howled, just making himself heard above the beating wings.

Apple was no longer smiling. "Leave this place, you monster." Her voice rang out strong and clear. "Know when you are beaten."

Scale tried to stand up and regain his previous cool, which was difficult when covered in slippery, smelly guano. He pushed his snout into Apple's face, and she tried not to flinch at his rancid breath.

"The Wolven belongs to Her Majesty's government," he hissed. "You will soon regret your actions, you mark my words."

Apple was in no mood for marking Scale's words or anyone else's. She commanded the birds again. Once more, the air became dark with magpies.

"Stop!" shouted Scale. "Call them off!"

"Get *out*!" screamed Apple.

Blood dripped from Lucas Scale's wounds as he staggered to his car. When it had disappeared, tires screeching down Camellia Lane, there was a stunned silence from all who had witnessed the attack of the magpies. It was broken by Jude.

"I think my parents have some information they need to share with us," she told Bill Beechgood grimly, *"and they had better hope that we find Nat and Woody before anyone else does."*

CHAPTER 20
EAST WOOD

"Get after them!" shrieked the guano-encrusted Scale. Vincent and Angelo glared at him with distaste through their polarized lenses.

"The whole place reeked of Wolven," Scale continued bitterly, banging his paw on the leather dashboard of the Hummer. "Gabriel Gruber made an enormous mistake underestimating the child," he growled. "In my experience it is always a great folly to do so. All children are willful, crafty, wicked, smelly . . ."

Vincent coughed politely, interrupting Scale's fervent musings.

"They can't have gone far, sir," he said. "My senses indicate an hour, at the most. They must have seen us arrive and sneaked off just before we got out of the car."

"What do you think Gruber will do to us if we go back

to the Halt empty-handed?" asked Scale. "Hmmm? Got any ideas? Because if you don't, *I* do."

Angelo stared straight ahead, Vincent down at the floor. They were getting fed up with Scale's attitude.

"Sniff them out and round them up!" screamed Scale, a crazed look on his misshapen face. He was furious with himself for walking into a trap. He should have known better. The woman had been a witch, and in a place like Temple Gurney he should have been prepared.

Angelo pulled the car over to the side of the road. As they climbed out, Scale scrabbled over to the driver's side, his orange eyes blazing with ill temper.

"What are you waiting for?" he yelled. "Go! Fetch!"

With that, he drove off, manically kangarooing down the road, leaving a cloud of dust in his wake. Vincent and Angelo stood there in the cooling heat of the evening in their designer suits and black patent shoes.

Vincent sniffed the fragrant summer air, wrinkling his lip slightly at the rich stink of exhaust fumes, blacktop, gasoline, and burnt rubber, all offensive to the over-developed olfactory system of the werewolf. Underneath lay more pleasing smells: wild marjoram, bird's-foot, summer anemones, and the pungent stench of wild garlic. Between the layers, in a kind of smell sandwich, was the scent of the boy and the Wolven.

If anyone had driven by, they would have been astonished, and not a little disturbed, to see two large Italian gentlemen removing their clothes and carefully folding them by the side of the road. If they had ventured within the outer perimeter of the woods, they would have been even more astonished to see the same two Italians crouching on all fours, grimacing and sweating as though in agony. Their bodies contorted as muscle and sinew stretched and writhed within their rapidly expanding skin. In turn, their skin, once smooth and tanned, became covered in long black hair. Then the Spaghetti brothers howled, long and hard. They were complete.

Hiding in the undergrowth off the side of the road, Nat had guessed correctly that the swanky government car he saw speeding toward his grandparents' house had contained the visitors Iona had warned them would come. He estimated, again with spot-on accuracy, that he and Woody had about an hour's head start before whoever was in the car would turn around and come after them. He'd allowed himself a brief moment of regret that he had not said good-bye to his mum, but he'd already grabbed his passport, some apples, and some clothing, stuffing them all in his backpack. He had one wrinkled ten pound note in British currency, and he had found a few euros in Apple's knickknack tray. Once he and Woody had hooked up with Crescent and the Howlers, they would be on their way to Eastern Europe.

When they reached the edge of the great East Wood, Woody's gaze rested on Nat, and he knew they had no choice but to get off the road completely. He hesitated. Woody sniffed the air, his ears and tail quivering, then he pushed his face between the dense trees. Nat watched nervously as the woods appeared to swallow Woody into its leafy depths. Taking a deep breath, he followed.

The first thing that struck him was the eerie silence, and the claustrophobic pressure of the trees, like they were trying to take him prisoner. No birds sang; there was no sound of small woodland creatures scurrying about their business in the undergrowth; none of the sorts of sounds you would usually hear in a woodland glade. It was monotonously green, featuring no other color except the faded brown of the unhealthy-looking tree trunks.

Nat glanced up, trying to peer through the green canopy to where tiny chips of blue fought their way between the branches of the trees. He wrinkled his nose at the dank, moldy smell; he couldn't imagine spending the night here. As soon as it got dark, they would head out again and, if they were lucky, find an empty barn to hide in.

But it seemed that Woody had other ideas. He loped slightly ahead, as if there were something up there he wanted to see. He kept his distance from Nat, glancing backward every now and then to make sure he was still following.

Nat's feeling of claustrophobia increased. In the unhealthy, humid atmosphere, his skin felt clammy and itchy, as if insects were crawling all over him. His backpack seemed to get heavier, and tiny pinpricks of sunlight flickered through the trees and into his eyes, almost hypnotizing him. Nat's eyelids began to droop.

"AAAAAAHHHOOOOWWWWWWWW!"
"OOOOWWWWWOOOOOH!"

The voices of the werewolves brought Woody back to Nat's side, his nostrils flaring, his eyes glowing, hackles as stiff as stalagmites.

"We're *so* dead!" cried Nat. "There's *two* of them."

Woody tore off ahead, then came back, then tore off again. Nat gave a small sob of defeat. He was all but done in. He doubted if Woody could take on two werewolves and win.

"I can't run as fast as you," he said. "You go on, I'll try my best to keep up."

Woody ran behind Nat, pushing him with his body, then ran up ahead, yipping and whining.

Nat took a deep, shaky breath. "I can't do it," he said sulkily. "I'm too tired."

"*A A A A H O O O O O W W W H H H o o o o o H H H o o a O O O O O O O O O O h!*"

It was as though someone had lit fireworks beneath Nat's feet. His tiredness evaporated at the chilling howl, and he took off behind Woody as fast as a ballistic missile. Branches tore at him, blood mixing with the sweat running down his face. He was aware of nothing except his heart pumping the blood around his body and the rhythm of his feet flying across the soft woodland floor. It beat a kind of tattoo within his brain.

He found he had got his second wind; now it seemed easier to run than it had been to walk. Nat had clicked into autopilot, running himself into a kind of trance. Woody's strength and energy seemed to infect him, pulsing through his veins and muscles, helping him keep up. He lost track of how long they had been running, and it wasn't until Woody's white coat took on a silver hue in the moonlight that he realized it had grown dark.

Up ahead, he thought he could see the vague, pale shapes of people waiting for them. They were all different sizes and appeared to be standing in a rough circle.

What now? thought Nat fearfully. *Surely Woody has seen them, too? Why is he running toward them?*

He saw Woody go and sit inside the circle. None of the shapes moved so much as an inch.

Nat didn't have the strength left to feel relief when he realized what the shapes were. Woody was sitting in a ring of ancient standing stones. One of the stones was much larger than its fellows, about the size of a tall man, with other, smaller rocks lying at its feet in an untidy heap.

Woody began scrabbling the smaller stones out of the way, before frantically digging in the mulch of leaves and dirt at the bottom, eventually revealing a narrow hole. It was more of a crack, really, between the stone and the earthy floor of the woods, about the same width as a small man. To Nat, it looked like the hungry maw of a giant's mouth.

"Oh, no! No way," said Nat, shaking his head violently. "I'm claustrophobic!"

"*AAAAAAAAOOOOOOOOOORRRRRRRRRR WHHHOOOOOOOOOOOO!*"

This time, the howls were closer. With no warning, Woody shot through the hole, disappearing out of sight.

Nat flung himself flat on his face, his head and neck fitting through the gap. He wriggled and writhed, but to no effect. He was too big! Panic rose in his throat, and then he remembered: He still had his backpack on!

He pulled himself out again, thinking that at any moment now, huge, sharp teeth would close on his legs. He shook off the pack and hurled it into the hole, then squeezed himself through. He tumbled forward into the darkness, expecting to land on Woody's soft, furry body. Instead, his knees and elbows scraped against sharp stones, making him yowl with pain. He didn't know which way was up; all his bearings were lost in his panic to get into the hole, away from their pursuers. Attempting to stand upright, he slipped and fell, kicking out with his feet to try to keep his balance. He eventually managed to stand, with his back propped up on a kind of rocky ledge, giving him some support as he peered into the blackness.

A sound made him freeze: an animal sound.

Oh, no, thought Nat. *They're in here. The werewolves are in front of us, not behind!*

"Ow! Get your foot out of my face!" shouted a familiar voice.

"Woody?" asked Nat joyfully, trying in vain to peer through the gloom.

"Who else did you think it was?" said Woody.

"I wasn't expecting you to change," said Nat, relieved. "That was quick."

"Getting better," said Woody modestly. "I'm so *smooooooth,* I can . . ."

Then total pandemonium broke out.

Something large and hairy rammed itself into the hole, clawing frantically at the musty air in the dark cave, trying to grab either boy. Nat opened his mouth in shocked horror as a giant misshapen paw slithered around his shoulders and hooked its claws around his neck, dragging him back toward the opening. They heard a primitive grunt of satisfaction as it pulled Nat nearer to the hole.

Woody positioned himself behind Nat, ready to fight for his friend. Eyes of blazing coal met Woody's. As Nat ducked, Woody's rigid index finger poked outward, straight into Vincent Spaghetti's eye. The werewolf howled in pain and fury, letting go of his prize as he pulled his paw out of the hole.

"Quick! Fill it up!" Woody shouted as Nat fell back, rubbing his tender throat. "Come *on*, we can't take the chance that they'll fit through!"

They scrabbled around on the floor to find stones big enough to block the hole, all the while expecting to see the slavering jaws of the werewolves appear.

When they were sure the hole was filled, they listened for any further sounds outside. There were none.

"They must have given up," whispered Woody.

"Thanks," croaked Nat gratefully. "That was *way* too close. I thought I was toast."

They managed to stand up without bumping their heads on the rocky ceiling. Nat tried to get his bearings. His eyes still hadn't adjusted to the darkness.

"Can you see anything?" Nat rasped.

"Yes, I think we're in a cave," said Woody.

"No way!" said Nat sarcastically. "I've figured that one out for myself, thanks."

Woody's face loomed scarily out of the darkness.

"Hey, your face is green," said Nat. "Are you OK?"

"So is yours," said Woody. "I think it's the lights in the walls."

"What lights?" asked Nat, puzzled. "I don't see any."

But gradually, as his eyes adjusted, Nat could see patches of luminescent material, glowing dully on the floors and ceiling of the cave.

"I think it's called phosphorus," said Nat, blinking. "That's better; I can see you pretty clearly now."

The cave was a miserable place. There was a *plinking* sound every now and then as water dripped from the ceiling.

"I want to get out of here," said Nat fervently. "It's one thing being lost in the open air, but here, it's like being buried alive."

Woody's nostrils flared expansively as he sniffed the air. "There's a passage at the end of this cavern," he said. "We need to walk quite a long way underground before we come to another entrance."

"How do you know?" asked Nat. "Can you smell it?"

Woody nodded, his eyes flashing with excitement. "I can *see* it! In my mind, I mean. Nat! We're underneath Helleborine Halt."

CHAPTER 21

OPHELIA MAKES A STAND

At roughly the same time Nat Carver had been staring down the barrel of Teddy Davis's BB gun back by the marina, Ophelia Tate was pacing the floor of her stuffy bedroom in Wookey Hole like a caged lioness.

Something's wrong! The bond she had shared with Woody hadn't been broken, even after she and Alec had betrayed him by selling him to Mick Smith and his young grandson. Her feeling of unease had led her to take an enormous risk, and she had tried in vain to contact Iona de Gourney.

Where was she? Ophelia had been calling her since the day before, but kept getting voice mail. It was very odd. Ophelia knew Iona rarely left Meade Lodge for long periods because of her animals.

When Ophelia's cousin, Professor Robert Paxton, had disappeared from the Proteus project, the money for

Woody's keep had kept coming for two years or more. When it ran out, Iona de Gourney had offered the Tates more money to keep Woody safe until she could safely smuggle him out of the country. Unfortunately, Woody was becoming more and more difficult to hide, and the Tates had been terrified that Gabriel Gruber and Lucas Scale would finally figure out that Woody was at their farm. They couldn't wait for Iona to come up with an alternative plan. In his haste, Alec had made things worse. Between them, they had placed Nat Carver in terrible danger.

When Woody had been at the farm, Ophelia sometimes got a funny, dreamlike sensation in her head as blurry images would start to take shape. Woody would show her with his mind where lost belongings were—her car keys or reading glasses—and she would sometimes know who was about to drive up the dusty track to the farm before they arrived, thanks to Woody. At least, she hoped it was Woody. She had heard from both the professor and Iona de Gourney that there were other creatures at Helleborine Halt dabbling in telepathy.

That morning, Ophelia had seen the crazed photograph of Woody in the *Reveille* and had run to show Alec. He had glanced at the picture briefly and shrugged.

"If the wrong people have seen that, he'll be caught!" cried Ophelia.

"If you mean them up at Helleborine Halt, he belongs to them anyways," said Alec morosely. "It's best all around he goes back to controlled conditions."

Ophelia stared at her husband in disbelief. "Best for *whom*, exactly?" she yelled. "And what about the other one? What about Nat Carver?"

Alec's bloodhound expression darkened. "Keep your voice down, woman. The Carver kid's got nothing to do with any of it."

"That won't make any difference to Scale, and you know it," spat Ophelia, then turned on her heel, red-faced and angry.

Later, just as Nat was proclaiming Woody's innocence to his family in Apple's kitchen, Ophelia stopped pacing her bedroom and slumped in front of her dressing table, gazing moodily into the mirror. She picked up her hairbrush and brushed her hair, still brooding about Woody and Nat Carver. As the brush slid soothingly through her blue-black hair, the room darkened, as though the sun had disappeared behind a cloud. The temperature dropped slightly, and Ophelia shivered involuntarily as a chill ran down her spine.

If Ophelia had ever doubted her bond with Woody, she couldn't do so any longer. The otherworldly sensation she sometimes felt when Woody was trying to show her something was so strong that she could feel his presence as if he were standing right beside her. She closed her eyes and opened her mind, and what she saw made her gasp in horror.

"AAAAAAHHHOOOOWWWWWWWW!"

"AAAAAAOOOOOOOOOORRRRRRRRRR WHHHOOOOOOOOOOOO!"

The howling jarred Ophelia's brain. In her mind, she could smell the meaty, animal smell before she saw them emerge like greasy smoke through the dense woods, sniffing the air for evidence of their quarry. In the twilight they stood: two identical orange-eyed werewolves, their eerie howls echoing through the forest, chilling the blood of whoever heard them. Ophelia watched through closed eyelids, slumped at her dressing table, breathing shallowly as the werewolves ran on tirelessly through the darkening woods. Up ahead, in the distance, Ophelia's mind made out two more figures: a boy and his Wolven friend, their feet flying over the woodland floor.

Half an hour later, Alec Tate stood in the doorway of the bedroom.

"What in the blue moon d'you think you're doing?" he asked Ophelia, a constipated look on his narrow face. Either she was going to a costume party or else she had gone as mad as a hatter. His wife was dressed in her old army combat gear (he noticed the pants were slightly strained in the seat area), and her face was blackened with what appeared to be soot. Her long black hair was pulled back into an eyebrow-raising braid.

Ophelia glanced at him, but wasted no time in answering. She dragged a large wooden chest out from under the bed, threw open the lid, and rummaged inside. With a triumphant grunt she pulled out something wrapped in an oily rag. She shook away the cloth and picked up the object, turning it lovingly from one hand to the other, as if she were welcoming an old friend. The revolver glinted dully in the evening light.

Alec gulped. "Now, now, Ophelia, don't be hasty," he said, backing away slightly.

She threw him a scornful look and pulled out two more relics from her active service days: an ancient, slightly sweaty pack of dynamite and a full field medical kit.

"I'm going back to Helleborine Halt," said Ophelia simply. "They've got Woody."

Alec looked confused. "No . . . no, he's with Mick Smith's boy, his grandson, how could he be . . . ?"

Ophelia cut him off. "He's in trouble!" she spat. "Don't ask me how I know, because you wouldn't understand. He'll die if I do nothing."

"You can't do anything on your own, woman!" shouted Alec Tate, gripping his wife by her camouflage-clad shoulders. "There's all sorts of nut jobs up at that insane asylum! Monsters, madmen . . ."

"Nat Carver is with him," said Ophelia softly.

Alec Tate's bloodhound face went white.

CHAPTER 22
HALLS OF HORROR

"But how can you remember Helleborine Halt?" asked Nat, exasperated. "I thought you were just a pup when you left."

"I didn't say I *remembered* it," said Woody patiently, his nostrils flaring. "Smell the stink of it! And listen. There's noises."

Nat strained his ears. He couldn't hear anything, apart from the *plink plink* of water as it dripped from the roof.

"Come on," said Woody. "We need to get out of here."

"Wait a minute," said Nat, a hysterical bubble of laughter in his voice, "haven't you forgotten something?"

"Don't think so," said Woody, puzzled.

Nat felt around for his rucksack, opened it, and rummaged inside. "Here," he said, "you might want these!" It was a pair of shorts and a T-shirt.

Nat relied on Woody to lead the way again. Although the phosphorus gave them some light, the bottom of the cave was strewn with slippery shingles, which made keeping their balance difficult. Nat was slipping and sliding on the loose scree, swearing to himself every time he slipped. He already had plenty of cuts and bruises from his flight through the woods and his struggle with the werewolf; he didn't want to add to his injuries.

It felt like they walked for hours; their arms and legs were stiff with tiredness and their heads bent at awkward angles from trying not to bang them on the ceiling. But at last the tunnel opened up, and a patch of welcome light was visible up ahead.

"Look!" said Nat in relief. "There's the way out."

"Not daylight," said Woody. "Don't get too excited; it's dark, remember?"

Woody was right. As they turned the corner the passage lost its greeny glow from the phosphorus and was lit by utilitarian halogens, like you would see in a factory or school. It had a dirt floor, on which stood various boxes and pieces of old office furniture.

"It looks like some sort of storage space," whispered Nat nervously.

Woody nodded. "This is the bottom level; another two above us."

"*There's* our way out!" said Nat, pointing to a door set in the roughly hewn rock. It was a heavy iron slab, with a window in the center. Nat tried to peer through to see what was on the other side, but it had been blacked out. He pushed it experimentally.

To their surprise it swung open on silent, well-oiled hinges. Bravely, Woody peered around the door to see what was on the other side. It was another corridor, lit with the same harsh lighting, and with many other doors set within the rock, all closed. Nat pushed open the nearest one and they both stepped inside. There was no one else in the large room — no one else *alive*, that was.

A soft light glowed from a desk in the corner. There appeared to be a great many podlike capsules suspended by some unseen means, looking as if they were hanging unsupported in midair. The pods were made of a clear material that allowed you to view what was inside, but Nat didn't think it was glass. He peered into one and recoiled in shock when he realized what it was. He tried to drag

Woody away before he, too, could see what horrors the pods contained, but it was too late.

In the nearest capsule was a tiny Wolven, barely the size of a cat. Its white fur floated dully, its face drawn into a frozen snarl as if it had died in pain.

Nat and Woody walked in sickened silence through the rows of pods. The poor, tortured creatures inside revealed the real story behind the Proteus project, and how badly it had failed.

"Is . . . is this how I will end up?" whispered Woody. "If they catch us, will I end up in one of those j . . . jars?"

"No!" cried Nat. "That's not going to happen. They won't get the chance."

"The werewolves who chased us," said Woody dully, "they'll know the tunnel leads here."

"Stop it," said Nat angrily. "Get a grip. If Proteus is beyond the police and the government, we'll go to the press. We'll get out of here and . . ."

"Sssh!" interrupted Woody.

"What?"

"Someone . . . someone's *coming*!"

BANG! BANG! BANG! The overhead lighting snapped on and the dim room filled with eye-wateringly bright halogen lights.

"Someone," said a harsh, guttural voice, "is already HERE!"

Nat's nightmares about Lucas Scale and the image Iona had shown them on the computer had not prepared him for the reality. Scale had appeared like a pantomime demon, seemingly from thin air. Nat's eyes were wide with disgust and horror at the sight of the rank creature that now stood before them: a vile werewolf hybrid walking upright, against all laws of nature.

"How wonderful to meet you at last," Scale purred, eyes glowing like two malevolent coals. "I have waited so long for this moment."

"Don't look at his eyes!" shouted Woody.

The expression on Scale's raddled face, still pitted and bloody from the magpie attack, looked uncertain for a moment; then he smiled.

"You've hurt my feelings," he simpered. "I never had any intention of harming you, Woody. We just did what we needed to, to get you back safely into our fold."

Nat stood rooted to the spot, still trying to believe this was for real. Scale had haunted his dreams for so long it was almost a relief to see him for what he really was: a vile, arrogant murderer. Nat made a bargain with himself: Whatever happened tonight, he wasn't going to be terrorized by this nightmare creature anymore.

"Cat got your tongue, boy?" Scale asked Nat. "Anything you'd like to say?"

"You're a monster," said Nat matter-of-factly, "and you stink."

Scale threw his head back and howled. When he had finished, Nat realized it was his way of laughing.

"I'll take that as a compliment," sneered Scale.

"How could you do this?" shouted Nat. "Woody's clan is wiped out because of you; they were the noblest creatu—"

"Save your venom for the real plunderers of *noble* creatures," snarled Scale. "We are *creators* here at Proteus, not destroyers. You want to talk about wiping out noble creatures? There are only one hundred and twenty-three tigers left in Nepal, thanks to common human poachers. Orangutans are now only found in Borneo and

Sumatra, due to man's disregard for their habitat."

"How can you say you're . . . you're *creators*?" asked Woody in disbelief. "Look at all these dead bodies!"

"Unfortunate," said Scale sorrowfully. "I admit, in the early days of Dr. Gruber's appointment, we had our disappointments. You can't have failed to notice my looks have . . . ah . . . suffered since some of the early experimentation. The sacrifices I have made are quite beyond the call of duty."

"So why did you do it?" asked Nat, interested despite himself.

Scale looked surprised. "Why? I would have thought that was obvious. Power, my dears. Power and riches beyond your wildest imaginings."

"What about Iona and Professor Paxton?" asked Woody suddenly. "Are they floating in pods somewhere? Have you killed them, too?"

Scale looked hurt again. "No, of course not," he said. "They are enjoying a reunion as we speak; they are perfectly well. But, boys, boys, boys. How we chatter. The night is still young, and Dr. Gruber is keen to meet you before daybreak."

He turned to the door; Nat and Woody hesitated.

"Come on!" cried Scale. "Walk this way. I'll show you to your room."

Nat swallowed another hysterical giggle as he watched Woody follow Scale. Even though they were in big trouble, Woody stuck out his bottom and made his legs go all bandy. In an attempt to cheer up his friend, he'd perfectly imitated Scale's unfortunate gait.

Lucas Scale led Nat and Woody through the labyrinthine bowels of Helleborine Halt, twisting and turning as if in a great hurry. There was a smell here that Nat recognized; it must have been what Woody meant when he said he could smell Helleborine Halt. It was the kind of smell that catches in the back of your throat. *The kind of whiff*, he thought, *that you smell in the lion house at the zoo.*

The noises were zoolike, too: the sound of restless animals pacing up and down; angry growls and feral grunts. Nat couldn't even bring himself to imagine what creatures were housed in these cells. As if Scale read his mind, he stopped outside one of them. The front of the cell was like an old-fashioned jail, reinforced with steel bars.

"Here." He winked an orange eye. "I believe you are acquainted."

He stood back to let Nat and Woody get closer to the bars. Despite Nat's reluctance to have Scale behind them (he kept imagining Scale's teeth folding into the back of his neck), his curiosity got the better of him. There was something lying on the floor of the cell; its sides heaving, its breathing harsh and irregular.

Nat moved forward until his nose was inside the bars, his pupils enlarging to accustom his eyes to the gloom. A large wolflike creature lay there, its eyes closed, seemingly asleep.

"A new recruit." Scale grinned, his eyes glowing like embers. "He's sleeping it off. The change comes about three or four hours after they're . . . er . . . *recruited*. Then they learn to regulate like the others."

Nat and Woody stared at Scale. Woody took a deep breath.

"How many others have you 'recruited'?" he spat.

Scale turned to face them, his expression sorrowful once more.

"It's a terrible compulsion I have," he said.

Nat glanced at Scale. He did sound quite remorseful; maybe they had been too hard on him.

"So how many?" asked Woody again.

Scale's eyes shimmered and gradually changed color from orange to molten red; they were quite beautiful. "Eleven," he admitted. "Five are almost ready for conversion to our special forces."

Nat began to feel a little dizzy; Scale's gentle voice sounded so comforting.

He watched as the wolf creature inside the cell shifted its head toward the door; maybe it could hear them. Its pelt was so finely blond that Nat had mistakenly thought it bald at first. Its half-open eyes were almost pure orange, the pupils tiny black pinpricks. Nat thought he had seen eyes like that before, only then they had been blue.

"Look at its eyes," he breathed. "They remind me of someone."

"Never mind its eyes!" cried Woody in surprise, pointing to the wolf's foreleg. "That's your watch!"

CHAPTER 23
REDEMPTION

The moonlit marina was deserted. Mick ran across the rickety boardwalk to where the *Diamond Lil* bobbed gently on her mooring. He was doubtful that Nat would have taken Woody aboard, but he had promised Jude he would search everywhere they might have hidden. As he expected, it was empty; there was nowhere for a boy and a large animal to hide. He paused at the cabin door, felt around in the darkness, and found what he was looking for. He locked up despondently and jogged back to Camellia Lane.

It was almost dark when he got home, and for the first time that summer, Mick felt a chill. There was another strange car outside the house, and Mick groaned inwardly. *What now?*

He was greeted at the door by Apple, her eyes red from crying.

"Thank goodness!" she cried. *"Hurry."*

Sitting at the kitchen table with Jude was a cowering Alec Tate. Mick was surprised; Alec Tate was the last person he had expected to see again. And by the way Alec was avoiding his gaze, this was going to be bad news.

"You'd better tell him everything," said Apple icily.

Haltingly, Alec told his story. Mick listened in silence as he spilled everything: from agreeing to hide Woody at the farm to Ophelia's strange vision. When he had finished, he glanced nervously at Mick and braced himself for a hiding.

But Mick's conscience was troubling him, too. He sat down heavily.

"I gotta take my own share of the blame," he said with a sigh. "A few years ago, I was up at East Wood doing a spot of poaching. It was a red moon that night, a harvest moon, and it was a cracker. The woods was all aglow: It was like the trees were alight. I can remember thinking it was a bit creepylike, as I was on me own. Then I heard something I don't never want to hear again, as long as I live."

"What was it?" asked Alec, agog.

"It was a bloody gert werewolf," said Mick. "A big black 'un, caught in a trap. It was making this horrible sort of keening sound, and it got right inside my head. I was all for shootin' it; puttin' it out of its misery. Then the blighter spoke to me. Good job I had me brown corduroys on! Anyways, I saved his foot, and he beggared off."

"Did you report it?" asked Alec Tate.

"Who'd-a believed me?" asked Mick glumly. "Things like that are best kept to yourself."

"I hope you realize you've put Nat in terrible danger by keeping your secrets," said Jude bitterly. "And you wondered why I couldn't wait to leave Temple Gurney! If anything has happened to him . . ."

"Woody's not a werewolf," said Alec. "He's harmless, even I know that now."

"I *know*!" shouted Jude. "It's not Woody I'm worried about!"

Mick hung his head. "Apple knew Woody was more than he seemed even before she discovered the tattoo. But you know how she has a gift for such things; I swear she knew he was harmless."

"Like I said, anyone can tell Woody isn't a werewolf," said Jude, exasperated. "You don't have to be a *witch* to know that." She glared at Apple, then turned her attention back to Alec.

"Ophelia's certain they've gone to Helleborine Halt?" she asked.

"I *told* you," said Alec, "she saw some sort of . . . vision in her mind. Saw 'em being chased through East Wood. An' she said what was chasing 'em *weren't human*. She's gone straight up there. Wouldn't wait, in case you didn't believe me."

Mick was standing now. "She armed?"

Alec flashed his dentures for the first time that day. "To the *teeth*."

Alec Tate came very close to redeeming himself that night. He organized the rendezvous with Ophelia, who was waiting for backup at the edge of East Wood.

Mick disappeared into the living room, reappearing minutes later with the pair of samurai swords that usually hung above the fireplace.

"Told you these beggars would come in handy one day." He winked at Apple and whirled them experimentally around his head. Pulling off his suspenders, he fashioned a rudimentary holster for them. Then he rummaged in the cupboard under the stairs and retrieved his snooker cue, grouping it with the emergency flares he had taken from the hold of the *Diamond Lil.*

"Shouldn't you wait for Bill?" asked Apple fretfully. "He's still trying to make some calls to London to get a search warrant."

Mick shook his head. "By the time he gets a warrant, it could be too late."

CHAPTER 24

BANGED UP

"I do hope you two young gentlemen don't mind sharing a room," purred Lucas Scale in his new, soothing tones. Nat and Woody looked at each other, confused.

What's he talking about? thought Nat. *What did I miss?*

Scale fixed them both again with his molten eyes. "On behalf of the Proteus project, I do hope you enjoy your stay. Do please let room service know if there's anything special you would like."

Nat found himself beginning to warm to Lucas Scale. *Maybe he's OK after all*, he thought. *Maybe I misjudged . . .*

"Look away!" howled Woody. It was too late. With supernatural speed, Scale reached out, hooked open the door next to Teddy Davis's cell, and shoved Nat roughly. He fell inside, crying out in pain as the side of his face struck the ironwork of the crude bunk bed. Before Woody could react, Scale had dragged him inside by the neck, holding him so tightly he almost lost consciousness. The whole procedure had taken just seconds.

Deprived of oxygen, his senses reeling, Woody took a moment to realize what had happened. As hard as he'd tried to fight it, as much as he'd tried to warn Nat, they'd both been tricked by Scale, who'd been hypnotizing them from the moment he'd found them in the pod room.

Woody jumped up and grabbed the bars, shaking the door.

"Let us out, you stinking monster!" he howled. "Let us go!"

"Sticks and stones," murmured Scale distractedly. "We'll talk again later. In the meantime, get some sleep. And I'll see you in your dreams."

Woody continued to shout and howl, calling Scale by a variety of rude names, using words he'd picked up from late night television programs on the less educational channels. He watched in despair through the bars as Scale disappeared out of sight.

Deep in the secure unit, Gabriel Gruber was ecstatic.

"Whatta guy!" he cried in admiration as he watched Scale imprison the boys live on the security cameras, in full digital color. Since they had emerged from the tunnel, he had been monitoring Nat Carver and the Wolven's progress enthusiastically.

Angelo and Vincent Spaghetti also watched, but not in admiration. They cringed in shame as they watched the two boys lose their futile struggle against Lucas Scale.

Gruber was too busy whooping and jumping up and down like he was on some sort of game show to notice Angelo's and Vincent's increasing unease.

"Take a bow, fellas!" He beamed. "You helped bring him home!"

Vincent and Angelo followed Gruber from the room, tight frowns on their handsome faces.

Had anyone been paying attention to the security cameras as they scanned every other sector in the facility at ten-second intervals, they would have seen a number of interesting sights. The cameras flipped from one room to the next, as if possessed. They zoomed in on the face of an old professor, his long gray beard rising and falling on his chest as he slept in his prison bed. They visited the locked room of a young blond woman of noble birth who did not sleep; instead she paced up and down, hoping for a miracle. They flipped out to the grounds again, zooming in on two smudgy patches of movement at the bottom left of the screen. If anyone *had* been monitoring the security cameras during those crucial ten seconds, they would perhaps have taken the time to investigate just what those patches were, but ten seconds passes quickly, and the cameras flipped off again to another location, starting their search from the beginning.

"Not much farther," panted Ophelia Tate. "We're looking for an old air-raid shelter."

She had briefed Mick Smith on the situation as thoroughly as an army general, and they both agreed they could not afford to wait for Sergeant Beechgood to obtain a warrant to search Helleborine Halt. If they were going to help Nat and Woody, they had to act fast, before it was too late.

Alec had declined to accompany Mick and Ophelia, staying to protect Apple and Jude. But after a few minutes fretting about his wife, he decided that more action was required. He leafed through the Yellow Pages and made a series of telephone calls that would have made Ophelia proud.

The shelter was one of the many disguised entrances to the tunnels under the Halt, and it was where Ophelia had last seen her cousin. Professor Robert Paxton had carefully placed Woody, then only a tiny white ball of fluff, into a cardboard box and handed it to her, sadness in his eyes. The tunnel had been in disrepair even then, and Ophelia was praying that it had not fallen in.

When they reached the small, brick-built shelter, it was padlocked. Mick Smith stood back in admiration as Ophelia Tate bludgeoned the lock with the butt of her revolver, then ripped the door off its hinges. Her eyes shining, she grinned in triumph at Mick, and without a word he followed her into the musty darkness.

"Phew, you're gonna have a big flasher tomorrow," said Woody as he helped Nat sit up.

"You mean *shiner*," said Nat, wincing as he touched the spot where his face had collided with the bed frame. "That went well. What are we going to do now?"

Woody shrugged glumly. "Dunno. What d'you think they're going to do to us?"

Nat shook his head in defeat. From where he was sitting it didn't look good, for him especially. Proteus had what they wanted, and he, Nat, was surplus to requirements.

Woody sat down next to him. He could smell Nat's fear and felt responsible.

"I . . . I could tell you a joke if you want," he said shyly. "It's really funny."

"OK," said Nat, brightening, "go on."

"Here goes," said Woody, taking a deep breath. "I used to be a werewolf, but I'm all right *nooooo*OOOOO OOOOOOOOOOO*ooooooowwwwwwwwwwwwww!*"

"That was *terrible*," said Nat in disgust, "and too loud. My head hurts."

"Sorry," apologized Woody. "Your turn."

Nat thought for a minute. "OK, I got a good one. A polar bear goes into the post office. He goes up to the counter and says, 'I'd like some . . . . stamps, please.' The post office lady says, 'Of course, but why the big pause?' The polar bear says, 'I dunno, I've always had them.'"

Woody looked puzzled. "I don't geddit."

Nat sighed wearily. "Paws?" he held up his hand. "Not *pause—paws!*"

"Nope," said Woody, shaking his head, "still don't geddit."

Nat struggled to his feet. "I promise I'll explain if we ever get out of here. Got any ideas?"

"If Scale comes back alone, we'll take him by surprise," suggested Woody.

Nat thought for a minute. "If you could change into Wolven form," he said, "you could knock him over, then we could make a run for it. What d'you think?"

Woody looked doubtful. "I could try, but I still can't always do it."

Nat grimaced. Woody was right: His control was improving, but how many times had it gone wrong? Nat remembered the half-boy, half-wolf occasion at the fair and, worse, the weird melting incident. He put his head in his hands in despair.

"Then I think we're done for," he said tiredly. "What else you got?"

As Woody thought for a moment, a small smile formed on his face. "There is something. . . ."

Nat looked up expectantly. "Go on."

"Remember I told you I learned most of what I know from TV and telepathy?"

Nat nodded impatiently. "Yeah, from *Jeopardy!* and *Who Wants to Be a Millionaire.*"

"There's another thing I found out I can do when I watch TV shows," Woody said, his eyes flashing topaz with excitement. "But they have to be happening at the same time I watch them."

Nat looked puzzled for a moment. "Oh, you mean *live* shows, like morning talk shows? Not a recorded program?"

"And like *Blue Peter.*" Woody grinned.

"O . . . K," said Nat slowly, "what are you talking about?"

"I made one of the cats on the kiddie show *Blue Peter* do something bad," said Woody guiltily. "I *puuushed* him with my mind."

At the mention of the *Blue Peter* cat, a big bell rang in Nat's brain. His eyes widened in amazement. "That was you?"

Woody grinned again. "Yup."

Nat's face split into an enormous grin, too, as he remembered the famous clip from a year or two back. It had been pure TV gold and had been on all the outtake programs, even making the nightly news. The horse-riding daughter of a minor member of the British royal family had appeared on *Blue Peter* with her Olympic gold medals. She had taken off her riding helmet and the *Blue Peter* cat had famously used it as a toilet. The presenters had lost control of the program, cracking up unprofessionally. The camera had loved it.

"Let's think about this," said Nat, trying not to get too excited. "You pushed my mind to see what would happen if I hadn't taken you away from Mr. Tate. You made the *Blue Peter* cat go wee-wee in Her Highness's helmet. Could you push Scale into letting us go?"

"I dunno," said Woody. "But I might be able to make him see things that aren't there, things he's really afraid of."

"How do you know what'll frighten him?" asked Nat, curious.

"I'm not sure yet," replied Woody, smiling. "But using tel . . . telepathy, I can find out."

Scale was flushed with success. He was one step closer to achieving his goal and one step closer to getting rid of Gabriel Gruber. How he detested him. The only reason he put up with him was because of Gruber's persuasive hold over the government officials at Whitehall. The Proteus project had been on hold for too long; with the return of the Wolven they could resume their experiments and their plan to provide the world's superpowers with an elite army of indestructible mercenaries.

Scale closed his orange eyes in rapture as he descended into the bowels of Helleborine Halt. Gabriel Gruber would be history in a few hours.

An eerie buzzing sound met him as the doors of the elevator swooshed open. Scale sniffed the musty air. *There it was again!* He frowned uneasily. It sounded like . . . *bees*. As he walked, bowlegged, down the corridor, Scale couldn't help noticing that the sound was getting louder. He shook his head; it was as though the noise was coming from the end of the corridor.

There can't be any bees here, he told himself. He had ensured that all Proteus staff had express orders to exterminate bees. *It was a bee-free area!* Scale checked his pockets frantically. *Where was his injectable adrenaline?* He was allergic to bee stings: If he was stung, his throat would close. He wouldn't be able to breathe without the injection. . . .

Scale forced himself to calm down. He couldn't hear the buzzing noise now; he must have imagined it. He gulped. Bees were the only thing that could frighten him. *And there are no bees here*, he told himself sternly.

Scale reached the cell where he had imprisoned the meddling Carver boy and his Wolven friend. He recovered his swagger as he peered through the tiny window in the door. The boys had taken his advice and gone to sleep, he noted with satisfaction.

Scale opened the heavy door cautiously. He was not so stupid as to just assume the boys really were asleep; it could be a trick. The Wolven stirred a little as the old door made a groaning noise. Scale cocked his awful head toward the Carver boy, who looked quite pale, save for the black eye he had sustained when he was thrown into the cell.

But what was this? Lucas Scale whirled around in panic. Through the open doorway, almost in military order, flew battalions of bees, billions of bees! *How had this happened?*

The buzzing filled Scale's head with white noise, his arms flailing wildly to stave off the bee attack. He was too busy to notice that the Carver boy and the Wolven had risen to their feet.

"Run!" howled Woody. *"Go, go, go!"*

Scale howled, too, with rage and confusion, as the two boys fled.

"Just fantastic," murmured Gabriel Gruber. "Willya look at that?"

The Spaghetti brothers watched the TV monitor as the two boys belted through the subterranean corridors of Helleborine Halt. Still outside the empty cell, Lucas Scale had clearly gone insane. He looked as though he were doing some form of inelegant break dancing.

"What's he *doing*?" wondered Angelo Spaghetti in fascination. "Is he . . . 'krunking'?"

"I think I smell a rat," said Gabriel Gruber happily. "The Wolven is behind this. He's made poor, ugly Lucas see something that isn't there!"

"Whatever it is, it's made him go berserk," said Vincent, amazed. "Look at him. He thinks he's under attack from something."

Gabriel Gruber frowned. "What are you thinking of?" he said to the Spaghetti brothers nastily. "Go fetch 'em. Teach the Carver kid a lesson, why don't you? Put him in the cell with the new recruit. That'll be entertaining."

The halogen lights in the maze of passages had been killed by Gruber. It was as black as midnight in a coal mine; Nat didn't stand a chance. Woody pulled him along, guided only by old memories and instinct.

When the Spaghetti brothers caught up with them, they were cornered. Gabriel Gruber watched in mild annoyance as Vincent Spaghetti dragged Nat Carver back to the cells. Gabriel flicked off the screen, bored with the boy's ranting; the Carver child was really of no importance now. As he waited for the Wolven to be delivered, he wondered idly what would happen when the new recruit woke up to find Carver in his cell.

CHAPTER 25
DEATH'S DOOR

The first thing Woody noticed when Angelo dragged him into the laboratory was that every single member of the staff, even the geekiest, lowliest lab assistant, was armed to the teeth. They ignored him, almost as if they were under orders not to acknowledge him. The second thing was that there were more pods. This time the sides of the containers flexed and bowed as though whatever was inside was stretching or, more worryingly, trying to get out. When he looked closer, he was relieved that none of the shapes seemed to be Wolven. From what he could make out, the creatures within were long and distinctly reptilian. Woody decided he didn't *want* to know what the pods contained.

Angelo handed him over to Lucas Scale, and then someone else in the room spoke.

"At last!"

Woody looked away from the pods and saw a man with extremely white teeth and girly blond highlights in his hair. He wore an immaculate lab coat, its tails flapping briskly as he came tearing across the floor, his hand outstretched to shake Woody's. Woody stared at the proffered hand in undisguised hatred.

"As you wish," said Gruber regretfully, dropping his hand. "Time for that later."

"Who are you?" asked Woody dully.

"I am Dr. Gabriel Wentworth Gruber," said Gabriel, smiling mistily, "and the last time I saw you, you were this big." He opened his beautifully manicured hands and used them to outline the size of a wolf pup.

"Drop dead," growled Woody. "You're crazy if you think you can get away with this."

Gruber frowned. "Get away with what, exactly? This isn't an episode of *Scooby-Doo*, you know," he said. "Everything we do here at Proteus is within strict government guidelines."

"How many boys does Scale kidnap and re . . . recruit to your sick project?" snarled Woody.

"Woody, who has been telling you these terrible untruths?" asked Gruber gently. "If it's who I think it is, all I can say is that she hasn't been herself since she sabotaged the Wolven DNA."

"Liar!" shouted Woody. "If you mean Iona, she's told us everything. Her only part in this was bringing my clan here."

Gabriel shook his head sadly. "Oh, Woody," he said sorrowfully, "did she tell you she left the project of her own accord, because she was upset at what was going on? Or, rather, that we summarily dismissed her? In fact, it was Iona's arrogance and complete disregard for living beings that made it impossible for her to carry on here. Her drive to succeed cost lives, and eventually her mind became so unhinged that it was necessary to pension the poor thing off."

Woody shook his head violently. "You lie," he said. "You're just twisting things to . . . to cover yourself."

Gabriel Gruber smiled. "It was Iona who killed your mother."

Woody reeled back as though Gabriel had pulled a gun on him.

"I thought that would grab your attention," said Gabriel, enjoying the look of devastation on Woody's face. "Mr. Scale here, he saw it all."

Lucas Scale nodded.

"I'm afraid it's true," he said with fake sympathy. "It was just after you were born. Iona went to take you away from your mother, and she turned very nasty. Technically, it was self-defense."

Woody said nothing. Then he spat straight into Scale's grinning face. "I *know* you are lying," he said, smiling feverishly. "It was here, wasn't it?"

Woody shook off Scale's grip. Scale went to grab him again, but Gruber put his hand up. "Leave him!" he ordered, fascinated.

Woody moved over to a long padded bench, like a hospital gurney without wheels. It had straps made of steel-reinforced mesh, presumably to wrap around the arms and legs of whoever was being examined or experimented upon. He put his hands on the bench, his face contorting as though with pain. His mother wasn't the only being to have died in this place. Images of the past thundered through his tired brain. He could feel the souls of all the

Wolven who had perished calling to him as he ran his hands over the fabric of the bench. He saw everything, everything he needed to see, and he wished he hadn't.

"It was *you*!" He looked straight into Gruber's eyes. "*You* killed her, not Iona."

Gabriel Gruber shrugged. "She attacked poor Mr. Scale, then she bit *me*. Badly," he added, looking Woody straight in the eye. "It *really* hurt, so I had her put down. It's what people do, when they're bitten by their pets."

Woody closed his eyes and *puuuushed*. In a seamless, fluid shift, his body shortened and shimmered out onto four legs. His shaggy head shifted into a Wolven muzzle, ears stretching into points, his body now covered in luxuriant gossamer fur that glowed under the harsh laboratory lighting.

Gabriel Gruber felt his feet lift off the floor as Woody sprang, knocking him over. Then Lucas Scale let his own change take over. Still smarting from the bogus bee attack, he welcomed the opportunity to teach the Wolven a lesson. He reared up and Woody faced him: Wolven to wolf. The lab assistants watched in terror as the deformed werewolf and the Wolven circled briefly, then lunged at each other, moving so fast they seemed to become a gray blur. They snapped and snarled, each trying to bring the other down.

Although not as strong as Scale, Woody was nimbler. He weaved in and out of Scale's bandy legs, snapping and nipping just above the paws. When Scale fell, he fell on top of Woody, taking him by surprise. He pinned Woody by the throat, and it became clear to Gabriel that he would have to intervene. Werewolves were virtually indestructible, but Wolven, Gabriel knew from past experience, were not.

With the aid of an electronic shark prod and a wire noose, two of the largest lab technicians managed to remove Scale from Woody. With the noose around Woody's neck, he was dragged and fastened to the same table his mother had died on. Morphing between Wolven and human, he howled for his lost mother.

The howls reached deep into the bowels of the Halt, where Angelo and Vincent waited for the elevator.

"This sucks like a vacuum cleaner, bro," said Angelo Spaghetti, shaking his head as he listened to Woody's heartbreaking howling.

"Yeah," agreed Vincent, "we had kids that age in our old lives. I'm outta here."

"Would you have hurt them?" asked Angelo, staring at his twin. "If we had caught them, I mean."

"I wasn't a bad man, was I?" asked Vincent.

His brother shook his head. "You were the best, bro."

"And that's the last order I take from Gruber," vowed Vincent.

"So what're we going to do now?" asked Angelo.

"Only one thing *to* do, bro," said Vincent, his eyes flashing amber. "How about we rip this place apart!"

Angelo grinned. "Now you're talking!"

The elevator landed with a shivering sigh, and the Spaghetti brothers waited for the doors to open.

"Get your hands up!" hissed a voice from above.

Angelo and Vincent peered upward to the hatch in the roof of the elevator. To their amazement, the camouflaged face of a woman peered back at them. To their further amazement, she had a revolver pointed straight at them.

"Unless you have a silver bullet in there, madam," said Vincent politely, "that gun isn't going to do you much good, I'm afraid."

"Try me," said the woman grimly.

Another head poked through. Vincent and Angelo looked amused.

"I'm guessing by your unorthodox arrival that you're up to no good," Angelo said with a smile.

"Stay back!" commanded Ophelia Tate.

"We're the good guys!" said Angelo. "And would I be right in guessing you're looking for someone special? Someone by the name of Nat Carver?"

Ophelia's eyes narrowed. "How do I know we can trust you?"

"I'm a lover, not a fighter." Angelo grinned.

"Never mind all that!" cried Mick. "Do you know where my grandson is?"

By the time Ophelia and Mick had lowered themselves through the hatch, the Spaghetti brothers had briefly reported the events of the evening, conveniently leaving out the parts where they had chased Nat and Woody.

"We'll get your boys out, then we'll raze this place to the ground." Vincent smiled as broadly as his brother. "Leave 'em all at death's door, and tell 'em where they can go."

CHAPTER 26
A VERY PSYLLI PLAN

Nat Carver's black eye was throbbing dully. His body felt like a lumpy old sack of wrenches and his head ached so much that even his hair seemed to hurt. The thing that had been Teddy Davis was still sleeping just a few feet away from him. Nat found he didn't care.

A familiar melancholy howl filled his head, rising and falling in pitch, a sound so desperate and familiar. *Woody! What were they doing to him?*

Nat got up painfully from the damp floor and tried to look out of the small hatch. The corridors were empty. Nat tried hurling himself at the door, hammering and kicking, but it was useless. He stood in the middle of the small cell, flexing his fingers and breathing deeply.

Nat closed his eyes and tried to picture Woody. If only he could somehow send his friend a message, to show him he was still here, still hoping a miracle would happen and they could get out of this terrible place. He tried for a few minutes, concentrating on Woody's face, but it was no good; the two-way thing wasn't going to happen. Then a thought struck him. He took a deep breath, tilted his head back, opened his mouth, and howled.

"*A A A A A A A A A A A A A A A A A A A hhh O O O O O O O O O O O O O O O O aaaroooooh!*"

Nat listened to his howl echo around the grim corridors of Helleborine Halt. He hoped that somehow, somewhere, Woody would hear it and know that Nat was still alive and rooting for him.

As the howl trailed off, Nat froze. Someone was groaning, *growling*, in the corner of the cell. Almost back in his human shape again, Teddy Davis was waking up.

"What the . . . ?" Teddy grumbled, trying to sit up. "Wass goin' on? And where's my clothes . . . *ow!*"

"Don't try to speak," said Nat. "There's been a slight problem with some mad scientists. Oh . . . and some werewolves."

Teddy was just about to say something else when both boys froze. *Footsteps!* Echoing footsteps in the rock corridors. Nat braced himself. The footsteps stopped out-side the cell and the hatch in the door slid open.

They had come for him. It was one of the twin were-wolves, the one who sported an eye patch. And he was smiling. Nat, rigid with fear, waited for the door to swing back. When it opened, he almost passed out.

Scale must have done more than hypnotize me, he thought, *or else I'm hallucinating.*

Outside, flanked by the two enormous Spaghetti twins, was his granddad. Also with them was a large woman who looked like a cross between a soldier and a superhero from a comic book. Nat thought he might as well go along with this dream as it was the best he'd had since arriving at Temple Gurney. He flew into Mick's arms.

"It's not a dream!" yelled Nat, dancing around his granddad. "You're really here! But how did . . ."

"Shhh," soothed Mick, holding both Nat's arms. "That will all have to wait for now, no time. Nat, this lady is Ophelia Tate."

Nat glared at the large woman coolly. "Oh" was all he could bring himself to say.

Mick shook his head. "We have Ophelia to thank for everything," he said. "Without her, I wouldn't even be here."

Nat eyed Angelo and Vincent warily. "Granddad, these were the men who came looking for us," he said, "and you'll never guess what? *They're werewolves!*"

"And they are here to help us find Woody," said Ophelia briskly. "You" — she pointed at Angelo — "what's the score down here, soldier?"

Angelo stood to attention. Ophelia had correctly recognized him as a former serving soldier in the Green Berets. "Eleven lycans in these cells, ma'am."

"What about letting 'em out?" Ophelia grinned. "Create a diversion? That'd give the boys upstairs something to think about."

Vincent's face fell. "With respect, ma'am, that's not a good plan."

"Oh?" snapped Ophelia. "And why wouldn't it be?"

"You humans would be ripped to pieces," said Vincent. "These werewolves are crazy, apart from the new boy." He pointed to Teddy, who looked confused. He didn't know he was a werewolf yet.

Ophelia considered. "We have the means to defend ourselves, as do the humans in the lab," she said crisply. "From what I know about werewolves, they retain some human faculties. We'll be fine."

Vincent looked doubtful, then remembered something far more chilling.

"See those?" he asked, pointing upward.

Everyone looked up. Set into the rocky ceiling were round, disklike objects.

"It's a sprinkler system," Vincent said with a shudder. "Since Dr. Gruber had some trouble a few years back, any escapees get doused with Ag. It's a terrible way to go: It makes us shrivel up and melt."

"What's Ag?" asked Mick, puzzled.

"*Argentum*," said Angelo, his lip curling at the thought of it. "Or, as it's called in English, silver. Molten silver chloride fired through the overhead water system. It would be like you guys taking a bath in sulfuric acid."

Nat was still hanging on to Mick's arm, terrified he would disappear at any minute.

"Granddad, please," he begged. "I just want to get Woody out of here."

"We can't just barge in and take him," said Mick, shaking his head. "And I need a minute to take in all this werewolf stuff, like who's on our side and who isn't. No offense," he added hastily to Angelo and Vincent.

"None taken," Angelo replied with a grin.

With his one good eye, Vincent had spotted the flares and matches that Ophelia carried in her belt.

"May I?" he asked, holding out his hand.

Ophelia handed them over, puzzled.

"You and I are going to test these downstairs," Vincent said, smiling mischievously. "As far as I remember, there aren't any sprinklers down there. If I'm right, it should start off the rest of my plan with a bang!"

Teddy Davis had taken the news surprisingly well. Angelo Spaghetti had explained as gently as he could that Teddy was going to have to shave more often, among other things. He wasn't very happy to be locked in again, but Angelo promised to come back for him. It was important that everyone play their part. They only had one shot at the plan. If it failed, they were dead.

"If we see anyone, pretend I'm hurting you," said Angelo Spaghetti through gritted teeth to Nat as they walked the rocky corridors.

"Ow! You *are* hurting me!" yowled Nat.

Mick followed, armed with the samurai swords, leaving Ophelia and Vincent to carry out Vincent's plan on the level below.

Downstairs, the werewolves were flinging themselves around in their cells, some flipping from human to wolf and back again, smelling danger as the volatile phosphorus ignited and exploded, giving off a strange, eggy stink, like brimstone. It was as though the very fires of hell were burning in the depths below the Halt.

In the laboratory, Woody's howls turned to sobs as he morphed back to human form.

Scale, also returned to some semblance of humanity, was able to remove Woody's restraints.

"Am I going to have any more trouble with you?" hissed Scale, pulling hard on Woody's arms, so hard they were threatening to pop out of their sockets. Woody shook his head, trying to blot out the pain.

"Come on now," coaxed Gabriel, "don't fight your destiny; think how you are helping your country, just like your ancestors helped theirs all those hundreds of years ago."

Woody spat out a cold laugh. "It's not the same!" he shouted. "You're creating monsters!"

"Perhaps not as revered as the Wolven clan," admitted Gabriel, "but more effective. No room for emotions or morals, you see. And now that I have international cooperation, they'll be for hire to anyone in the world. Anyone who can afford them, of course."

He moved across the room to one of the milky pods, gesturing at Scale to drag Woody with him.

He poked the nearest pod hard, like an inquisitive child at the zoo. "Let me introduce you to the Psylli clan," he said. "*P-S-Y-L-L-I.* The *P* is silent, by the way. They live in trees usually, and when in human form they're almost as ugly as Lucas here. But when they metamorphose into snakes, they are the leanest, meanest killers I have ever come across in my entire career. They team the deadly bite of a taipan with the grip of an anaconda; I've seen these slippery little suckers swallow a hippo and regurgitate it in twenty minutes flat. The other benefit, from our point of view, is that they can blend into the background like a chameleon, contorting into shapes undetectable by any enemy, anywhere."

Still held in a viselike grip by Lucas Scale, Woody peered closer into the milky depths. *WHACK!* Two fangs tried to gain purchase on the slippery side of the pod and bite their way out. Woody didn't even flinch. He grinned at Gabriel mockingly.

"The things in these jars look like a joke," he said. "They look like they couldn't fight their way out of a paper bag *or* one of those pods. When were you hoping they will be ready?"

A shadow passed over Gabriel's handsome face.

"When are they going to be ready?" repeated Woody. "D'you want to phone a friend or ask the audience?"

Gabriel Gruber regained his composure. "By the end of this year, the first Psyllis will be exported for use in the field," he said firmly. "Obviously they won't be as sophisticated as the Wolven hybrids, but they'll serve a purpose on more covert operations."

"But you don't *have* any Wolven hybrids now, do you?"

taunted Woody. "They're all dead, thanks to you."

"That really is of no consequence," scoffed Gabriel.

"You better get a move on, then," continued Woody. "It'll be the twenty-second century before you work it all out!"

Lucas Scale coughed uncomfortably.

"Oh, we'll do it, all right!" cried Gabriel. "You are our Grail, our last chance to create another legend. The original Wolven were weaklings compared with what we are going to achieve."

Woody shook his head. "But the original Wolven didn't kill anyone. They were supposed to make things better, not worse."

"Animals have always been used in war," Gabriel Gruber declared with a grin. "Dolphins, horses, dogs, even pigeons. They're expendable."

"I don't even know what that means!" shouted Woody. "But if you want killers, just use those horrible snake people."

"To get back to the point, dear dog breath," sneered Gruber, "we might not have any *live* Wolven hybrids, but we have learned plenty from your little dead friends downstairs. Enough to know that cells taken from your brain stem are going to — Wha . . . what was that?"

A muffled noise came from below and the room vibrated and shifted just a tiny bit. Woody grinned wolfishly. "Looks like you might have something else to worry about," he said.

Gabriel snapped his fingers at Lucas Scale. "Get this Wolven trash out of my sight. Then check the cameras and find out where those blasted Spaghetti brothers are."

Another trembling bang, this time a good deal louder.

CHAPTER 27
SILVER RAIN

The Prime Minister was extremely chuffed. Earlier, he had thrashed the Chancellor of the Exchequer at golf for the second time in two weeks, and he was owed two thousand British pound notes for his wins.

Although he wasn't usually allowed a rich snack before bedtime (but his wife would never know, she was fast asleep), he had cause to celebrate. Gleefully he spread peanut butter and stacked marshmallows onto two slices of brown bread, added a layer of salami, and covered it all in maple syrup. He pressed the slices together and carefully placed the sandwich on his special panini machine. He could barely wait as the delicious aromas wafted up, making his mouth flood in anticipation.

When the sandwich press beeped, he lifted the lid, and was baffled when it continued beeping.

He frowned. He double-checked that he'd switched off the machine, but still the beeping didn't stop. Confused, the Prime Minister lifted up the toaster to look for an explanation. *Ah, wait a minute!* The beeping was coming from another part of the room. He cocked his head to locate the source, then groaned deeply.

This pager was different from his other four pagers. This pager went off for one reason and one reason only. He took a last, longing look at his sandwich, then dialed a secret code into his phone. Almost immediately it was picked up by a man named Quentin Crone, his new head of MI5, the British secret service.

"I'm sorry to bother you, sir," said Crone's rich baritone voice, "but I'm afraid we have a crisis at the research laboratory in Helleborine Halt. I've had a phone call from a local farmer; apparently some people have got in and are letting the animals loose. Probably animal rights activists, but my controller in Whitehall is very worried, very worried indeed."

The Prime Minister groaned again. "What color crisis?"

"A red one, sir," said Crone. "I'll pick you up in five."

In the bowels of Helleborine Halt, the phosphorus was going off like clumps of small but effective bombs.

The security cameras continued to whirl like dervishes, relaying their ten-second snippets all around the Halt: from the werewolves, now fully alert, nostrils flaring at the smell of danger and phosphorus; to the laboratory, where Dr. Gabriel Gruber was teetering on the edge of another tantrum.

"Have you found those twins yet?" he shouted at the surveillance cameras.

The cameras flipped obligingly to a beautifully distinct color shot of Angelo Spaghetti and Nat Carver approaching the laboratory. Gabriel stared at the screen in pure shock. Behind Angelo and the Carver child there was a strange man. Disturbingly, he appeared to be armed with two enormous swords.

The worst enemies are always those with nothing left to lose, and Gabriel, although absolutely barking mad, was not a stupid man. When he had calmed down enough to assess this new and rather worrying situation, he realized with sickening clarity that the Spaghetti brothers and the Wolven fitted into this category perfectly. For some reason, which he had never been able to fathom, people became very unreasonable at these times. He took a deep breath and told himself things were going to be just fine. When the uninvited guests burst through the doors, he was gratified to note they looked scared witless.

"OK," drawled Gabriel, smiling, his hands outstretched as if in welcome. "I'm sensing this is some kind of mutiny?"

Angelo Spaghetti ignored the question. "Dr. Gruber," he said formally, "in approximately sixty seconds, your laboratory will be filled with slavering werewolves. This is your last and only chance to remove yourself and" — Angelo threw a look of contempt at Scale — "your staff."

"My dear Angelo . . . ," started Gabriel. He was interrupted by a violent explosion from below, which made him grip Scale's arm for support.

"Listen — that's your cellars blowing up!" shouted Nat. "Pretty soon the fires will reach the next level."

"You really *are* beginning to annoy me," said Gabriel, the ugly vein beginning to throb in his temple. "Why couldn't you just have stayed at home and played with your toys like a normal kid?"

"Because Woody is my best friend!" shouted Nat.

"Correction." Gabriel grinned. "Woody *was* your best friend. Past tense, I'm afraid."

"He's lying," growled Angelo. "He wouldn't kill the sole surviving Wolven. But the kid's right, Gruber; the fires have started to creep."

"Then the sprinklers will kick in," replied Gabriel, still grinning maniacally, "and you, Angelo, will have signed your own death warrant."

Almost as soon as Gabriel stopped speaking, the werewolves started their eerie howling. The louder it became, the more the grin on Gabriel's face shriveled into the tiny, unappealing shape of a cat's bottom. The werewolves were close, their howls almost joyful. The sound rang around the Halt, shaking the rafters. Iona, in her locked quarters, could hear it, and she felt a wild hope in her heart. Professor Paxton awoke from his drugged sleep and thought of freedom for the first time in three long years.

Courtesy of the security cameras, everyone in the lab was treated to the visuals as a pack of crazed werewolves streaked through the corridors like deadly smoke, drawn by one thought: to destroy their tormentors. Scale and Gruber looked at each other in bewilderment as the desperate beasts flung themselves against the laboratory doors, knocking over equipment and computers, screens imploding as they hit the floor. Personnel ran screaming out the door or shrank back in horror as the werewolves stood in the middle of the room, forming a semicircle of bared teeth, drool dripping from their open mouths.

Gabriel Gruber's unhinged mind tried to assess the situation. *WHAT HAD HAPPENED TO THE AG RAIN?*

As the werewolves raised themselves on two legs and began to advance toward him in a solid wall of teeth and fur, Gabriel pushed one immaculately manicured hand through his tastefully highlighted hair. "Hey, guys, wait a minute . . . LUCAS, WILL YOU HIT THE RAIN ALREADY!"

Scale fumbled for the fail-safe handset, finally registering that the Ag rain had failed to start automatically when the werewolves had been released.

"HIT IT!" screamed Gruber.

The doctor closed his eyes in relief when the Ag rain spluttered, then fired out of the overhead devices, down onto the werewolves, making them clutch their heads in pain and terror, their fur singeing where the liquid silver touched them.

Then, abruptly, it stopped. There was complete silence in the lab as slowly the werewolves realized what had happened. They shook the droplets of silver rain from their fur like giant shaggy dogs and continued their menacing advance.

"Wha . . . ?" uttered Gruber, looking at Angelo Spaghetti in uncomprehending dismay.

"Vincent disconnected the supply," said Angelo. It was his turn to grin now.

"B . . . but w . . . what about the backup tank?" stammered Gruber.

"I believe he may have drained it," said Angelo, starting to enjoy himself.

"SHOOT THEM!" screamed Gruber, his handsome face a mask of terror and disbelief.

The few remaining lab technicians stared as if they were baby rabbits caught in headlights. They looked in unison from Scale and Gruber to the wall of werewolves and back again, like spectators at a tennis match. Then, as one, they legged it out of the room.

Gabriel Gruber glanced around the laboratory wildly. His escape route was barred by the furry mass of the werewolves that had closed ranks after the technicians' panicked exit. There was nowhere to run. As the werewolves reached Gabriel Gruber, the expression on his face was one of dawning realization. He was going to die. But he still had so much to offer! He felt himself being lifted up high by strong, clawed paws, and for one mad, vain, self-satisfied, smug, exhilarating moment, he allowed himself to think he was being held aloft like a hero. But it was only the werewolves' way of playing with him, like cats with a mouse. Gruber was flung up to the ceiling. When he hit the floor, his former prisoners pounced on him, greedily and without mercy.

Lucas Scale never missed an opportunity. While everyone's attention was absorbed by the shredding of his former colleague, he vowed revenge on the Carver boy. In the name of the Proteus project, he had been disfigured beyond all reason, and now his dreams of glory were rapidly dispersing, all because of that stinking, self-righteous little kid! He threw Angelo roughly across the room and turned his attention to Nat Carver, getting ready to spring.

Mick, guessing the hideous creature's intentions, raised his samurai swords above his head and charged. Scale, his eyes igniting as if on fire, grinned, baring his teeth in a sick smile of welcome.

"Granddad! *No!*" screamed Nat, as Scale viciously ripped the swords out of Mick's hands and grabbed him by the throat, his foul claws raking into the soft flesh. Angelo, stumbling to his feet, his hair still smoking from the Ag shower, tried to tackle the savage brute, but Scale's superior strength won. He kicked Angelo away like a soccer ball. Nat ran toward Scale, who turned his full attention to him, eyes flashing almost lovingly.

As if in slow motion, Scale received Nat into his outstretched arms and savagely fastened his blackened teeth deep into his throat.

CHAPTER 28
ALTERED

The monsters controlling the doomed shape-shifting Proteus project were dead. The pack of werewolves was making short work of dispatching their late tormentor, Dr. Gruber, and the loud bone-crunching and slurping noises were enough to give anyone indigestion.

The rescue by the unknown intruders had been carried out with admirable precision right through to the end, when, following his attack on Nat Carver, Lucas Scale had been felled by a single silver bullet from Ophelia Tate's army revolver.

Vincent and Angelo Spaghetti had quickly and efficiently removed the injured, including the young Carver boy, and left the scene, but Ophelia had one last task to complete before leaving the Halt. She and Mick had agreed that her last duty would be to put the project's other victims out of their misery. The risk that they might be recaptured and used in other experiments was just too great, not to mention the terrible danger to the public.

On her way back to the others, Ophelia had found the Halt's arms room and stocked up on silver bullets. Now, swiftly and silently, so as not to alert the snarling werewolves, she backed toward the open door.

"Shoot first, ask questions later!" barked the Prime Minister.

Quentin Crone, the head of MI5, stared at him. "With respect . . . ," he began.

"*Do it!*" The Prime Minister stared resolutely ahead. "Damage control, Crone, that's all we can do here tonight."

Crone glanced at the two other SA.330 Puma helicopters flanking them, waiting for orders. An eerie orange glow emanated from Helleborine Halt and stinking, pale green smoke billowed from the windows on the lower floor as the phosphorus continued to combust.

Crone had not had long enough to assess the situation; he was entering unknown territory. Fully briefed on the Proteus project during the brief helicopter journey from London, he had been sickened when he learned the full extent of the atrocities carried out by Gruber in the name of science. He'd had no idea there were *werewolves* involved.

An eerie sound carried on the wind made him shiver: a low, mournful howling, faint at first, then louder, as whatever was making the noise crept closer. Then Crone was aware of another sound as gunshots pierced the night air.

Using the laboratory door as a shield, Ophelia Tate had time to fire five rounds of the finest filigree silver bullets, scoring direct hits each time before the surviving werewolves came for her. Slamming the heavy door behind her, she sped through the smoke-filled corridors, expecting to feel the hot breath of the werewolves on her heels as she ran wildly for the elevator, which would take her to the safety of the upper levels.

The fires in the labyrinth were creeping higher. A buildup of gases caused an explosion, combusting toward the elevator shaft where Ophelia had been headed. She knew her chances of surviving the next few minutes were almost nil. If she stayed below, she risked being the second course for the remaining werewolves, but if the elevator caught fire while she was in it, she would be baked like an aluminum foil–wrapped potato.

"AAAAAAAHOOOOOOooooooooowahhhhhhhhhh!" A triumphant set of howls made up her mind for her; the pack had managed to break down the lab door. She stabbed wildly for the button on the elevator.

"Ow!" she yelped. It was red-hot! *Had the fire reached the elevator shaft?*

She cried out in relief when the elevator doors at last slid open. Jumping inside, she hit the button again to close the doors. This time nothing happened. *Oh please, oh please,* she prayed. She was still hitting the buttons when the corridor darkened. Ophelia held her breath as the dreadful silhouettes of the six surviving werewolves appeared on the wall just before they crept around the corner toward her, snarling and slavering, maddeningly slow as they stalked their prey. She slapped the button one more time in desperation.

"YES!" She punched the air, almost weeping as the doors closed. Her luck had held; she had a chance!

• • •

The Puma helicopters crouched on the lawns of Helleborine Halt like giant mosquitoes. Crone gave the signal for the searchlights to be trained on the mansion, and the night sky lit up with cold clarity, illuminating the front entrance. When it seemed there were no more human survivors, Crone had agreed with the Prime Minister that it would be just as well to let the werewolves perish in the fires. But then somebody had reported there had been two children held in the bowels of the Halt, and everything had changed.

There was movement from the main door. Someone was coming out. Crone watched as a well-built, dark-haired woman with a blackened face half fell, half jumped down the steps to the gravel drive. She was followed by something Crone would have nightmares about for the rest of his life. These werewolves had been altered beyond his wildest imagination. They ran upright, on two legs, not four. They stood almost ten feet tall, their glowing orange eyes feverish with hate, their muzzles drawn back from their dripping fangs, making a keening, howling sound that remained etched in Crone's brain for eternity.

Smoke billowing from Helleborine Halt was making visibility difficult. Quentin Crone tried to give the special services the order to fire, but his breath caught in his throat. He could make out the determined face of Ophelia Tate as she sprinted toward the helicopter, bravely trying to outrun the six snarling creatures who were closing in on her. Then, mercifully, although no order had been issued, shots rang out. Four of the werewolves took high-velocity silver bullets in the chest and were sent flying.

Crazed and confused, the two remaining werewolves turned toward the helicopter where Crone sat with the gibbering Prime Minister. As they stole menacingly toward the cockpit, Crone pulled himself together. At exactly the right moment, he hit a switch on the copter's dashboard. The rotor blades whirred into life. He closed his eyes as blood splattered across the glass bubble of the windshield, almost, but not quite, obliterating his view. Quentin Crone had already decided to hand in his resignation before the werewolves' severed heads hit the ground.

CHAPTER 29
WORLDS COLLIDE

He could feel the strong sun on his upturned face as they delivered him to the homebound ship. Rivers of blood had been shed and many brave men had died horrific, lonely deaths, in this far-off, alien land. And now, at long last, it was all over.

Mortally wounded, he was going home.

As he hovered in the dim world between life and death, he was aware of someone else in the cabin with him.

"Wha . . . ?" he rasped, his throat feeling ragged and raw, as though it had been ripped open.

"The Wolven brought you," soothed a woman's voice. "Drink this, 'tis rose water."

The heady, beloved smell of English roses invaded his senses. He struggled to lift his head, eager to sup the hot liquid. When he had drained the cup, his cares fell away, and he laid his head down on the soft, snowy pillow.

"May the heavens bless you," said Iona.

In the darkened room, Nat Carver felt as though his throat had been torn apart. He tried to lift his head from the pillow, but it hurt too much. It felt like the top of his skull had been hacked off, then stuck crudely back together with lumpy, ineffective glue. His mouth no longer felt like various small animals had curled up and died inside because, bizarrely, all he could taste was roses. An angel had given him the drink, but she was gone now. *Had he been on a ship? He was going home: Where was that?*

He slept again. Beside him on the huge bed lay a delicate gray-and-cream guardian. She cracked open one lapis lazuli eye to check if her ward was still asleep. She stretched on the luxurious quilt, glad that at last it had been safe to come out from under the bed.

On the second day, Nat's memory still drifted like a small boat, bobbing on the ocean. Other people had come, some with familiar voices, sounding worried and sad. Everything hurt.

It was dark. The candle at the side of his bed gave little light. His gaze drifted to the corner, where he could see the black outline of a person. He gasped. Two eyes glowed out of the darkness. Then it all came back to him.

Scale! He had been bitten by the foulest, most mottled, rotten, stinking creature ever to set foot on earth. Now he, too, was unclean, and there was the creature waiting for him in the corner of the room.

Nat started to flail. "No!" he cried. "I'd rather be dead than like you!"

The shape rose from the chair in the corner and rushed to the side of the bed. In his struggle, Nat pulled out the tubes he had sticking into his forearm, smashing some bottle onto the floor in the process.

"Nat, stop! It's me, Woody. Scale is dead. He can't hurt you anymore."

Nat stared at the strange boy by his side. "But he bit me," he croaked. His hands traveled to his throat, which was wrapped with a thick bandage. "I'll be like him."

Woody shook his head, trying to get through to his friend. "No, no, Nat, you won't, I promise!"

• • •

On the third day, Nat opened his eyes again. There was a large white Wolven snoring at the bottom of his bed, and the angel was back. She pushed his sweaty hair off his face.

"No need to ask how you feel," Iona said with a smile. "You look terrible."

"I saw you in my dream," he whispered. "We were on a boat, and you gave me a rosy drink."

"Did I?" Iona asked, still smiling. "Are you sure it was me? No, don't try to speak, you've suffered a bad injury to your throat; you nearly died."

"Where . . . ?"

"You're at Meade Lodge," said Iona brightly, "and *so* honored. Generations of de Gourneys have died in this bed!"

Nat closed his eyes. *Whoo-hoo, yeah, I'm honored*, he thought weakly.

"Woody hasn't left your side," said Iona, "not even to eat."

Nat smiled for the first time.

"Woody told me you remembered Scale biting you?" asked Iona.

Nat gave an almost imperceptible nod, and groaned.

"Hush now. Lucas Scale is dead," soothed Iona.

"And I have tainted blood," whispered Nat. "I'll be a werewolf, an outcast, like Vincent and Angelo."

Iona shook her head. "Ophelia saved you; she saved you twice over."

Nat squinted his eyes at Iona, trying to comprehend. "How?"

"When the werewolves turned on Gruber, Scale decided that if he was going to die, he was going to take you with him. He didn't want to *taint* you, Nat, he wanted to *kill* you!"

"Then she should have let me die," said Nat bitterly. "I survived a werewolf attack; everyone knows what that means."

"Let me finish," said Iona. "Ophelia shot him through his wormy heart, and then everything went crazy. The special services arrived: helicopters all over the grounds, personnel trying to decide whether to stay and face the music. Vincent found us, Professor Paxton and me, and we wiped the security camera footage. When we brought you back here, you'd already lost pints of blood."

Nat groaned. "I can't remember anything after his teeth . . ."

"Ophelia got you on a drip less than forty minutes after Scale had savaged you," said Iona. "She transfused Woody's Wolven blood into your veins. And, Nat, it worked! If it hadn't, you would have changed within three hours. The purity of the Wolven's blood sterilized the taint of Scale's."

Nat remained silent.

"Even if it hadn't worked, you would *never* have become like Lucas Scale. He was, thankfully, one of a kind. A horrible kind!" Iona added reassuringly. "Don't forget there are good, brave werewolves, too — like Angelo and Vincent."

Nat narrowed his eyes again. "And Crescent and the Howlers?"

Iona nodded. "Come on, what's the worst that can happen?" She grinned. "You know, maybe you'll have a few Wolven traits."

Nat appeared to think about it for a moment. "I guess. . . ."

"Ah, you had them anyway," said Iona. "You're one of the bravest people I've ever met."

Nat smiled at last. "You think?"

"I *know*," said Iona, green eyes shining.

"There's just one thing I'd like to ask," croaked Nat. "It seems like years ago, but when you said you were going to show us some *real* magic, what was it?"

Iona hesitated, then took a deep breath and took his hand in hers.

"I was going to hide you both in another time, where *no one* would find you."

"Was it a dream, when I was on the ship?"

Iona shook her head. "Sometimes you go *over*."

Nat's eyes opened wide. "Like when I flipped over into the past before? When I saw Richard the Lionheart?"

Iona nodded. "At times of great stress, worlds sometimes collide, get mixed up. Sir Will de Gourney received an arrow to his throat at the end of the Third Crusade, which nearly killed him, just as you nearly lost your life when Scale tore your throat. You and Sir William were linked because of the chronicle, and sometimes coincidences like that can affect our time line, and they clash."

"But what about you?" asked Nat. "You *were* there, weren't you?"

Iona lowered her eyes. "Maybe I belong there," she said.

Nat's bloodshot eyes widened. "You're not a *ghost*, are you?"

Iona put her hand on Nat's forehead. "Do I feel like a ghost?" she asked.

"Well, no," said Nat, "but . . ."

"I belong firmly in this century," she said briskly, "and Sir Will is a valued ancestor. Now go to sleep for a while. You have visitors coming later who will want to see you."

CHAPTER 30

BLOOD BROTHERS

"Good gawd, boy, you gave us a right old scare!" cried Mick as he limped into the room a couple of hours later. He was wearing his best visiting-the-sick beret, which was puce to match his beard. He also sported a bandage similar to Nat's, due to the injury he'd received from Scale. Apple and Jude had brought Nat some books, and sat on the end of the four-poster bed, making a fuss over Clawdia.

"Those Spaghetti brothers!" said Mick in wonder. "They were amazing."

"Nat, can you forgive us for doubting you?" asked Apple. "Especially me. I knew Woody was connected in some way to Helleborine Halt, but he wasn't anything like any werewolf I'd ever known!"

"Don't worry, Nan," Nat answered with a grin. "He's nothing like any werewolf I've ever known, either!"

"Helleborine Halt is virtually gutted," said Jude gravely. "There'll be no more evil deeds done there, thanks to Vincent and Angelo."

"What happened to the other werewolves?" asked Nat.

The silence confirmed his fears. Nat closed his eyes. "They're dead, right?"

Iona took his hand. "There was no alternative," she said. "They had a taste for human blood. If they had escaped, they would have caused chaos. If they had been caught . . ." Her voice trailed off. "We couldn't take the risk."

"But it wasn't their fault!" cried Nat. "Surely they could have been saved?"

"It was too late to undo the damage," said Iona softly. "They'll always be the innocent victims in the story of the Proteus project. Ophelia put her own life in terrible danger in order to put them out of their misery. She's a remarkable woman. The only justice is that the people responsible are dead, too, and I have it on good authority that the families of the missing will learn the whole story."

Remembering the werewolves and what they had endured cast a shadow over the gathering, and Nat was glad when Iona ushered everyone out of the bedroom, leaving him and Woody to doze in the darkening shadows.

The next day brought a more cheerful mood and more visitors for Nat and Woody. Nat could smell his next visitor before she arrived. It was Crescent. His senses seemed to have gone into overdrive. He wondered if it was his new Wolven blood. Or maybe it was because she had brought him a bunch of bedraggled yellow flowers that smelled so strongly of cat pee, they made his eyes water. Alongside her, looking lean and fit, complete with designer eyewear, were Vincent and Angelo Spaghetti.

"I'm *superbummed* you and Woody aren't coming with us," Crescent declared dramatically, tossing her flaming red hair. "The Spaghetti twins are coming instead, just for a vacation. When you're better, your dad says we can all meet up in Paris, special guests of John Carver's Twilight Circus of Illusion."

In the Italian style, Vincent and Angelo each kissed Nat and Woody on both cheeks.

As he reached the door, Vincent hesitated. "There's an old proverb our Spanish brothers live by," he said thoughtfully, as though he had just remembered it. "'Live with

317

wolves and you learn to howl.' I think, my friends, that you have learned this well."

Ophelia was the next visitor.

"I can't undo my part in what Alec and I did," she said, "but whatever happens now, at least you and Woody will always have each other's friendship."

Nat and Woody returned her bear hugs and Ophelia's face lit up with a radiant smile. All the hard edges dropped from her face, and for a moment she was beautiful.

"There . . . there's somebody else who wants to say good-bye," said Ophelia mysteriously.

Even before the door opened, Nat knew who the visitor would be.

"All right?" said Teddy Davis awkwardly. Like Angelo and Vincent, he wore tinted sunglasses to hide his strange orange eyes, although, thought Nat privately, Teddy's glasses weren't half as cool as the designer ones the Spaghetti brothers wore.

"I . . . uh . . . I came to see how you're doin', and to return this," he said nervously, holding out the watch he had taken from Nat.

Nat smiled. "Keep it," he said.

Teddy Davis grinned back. "You sure?"

"Sure," said Nat.

Teddy looked uncertain for a moment, then held out his hand. "Shake on it?"

The three boys shook on it. Then they looked at each other awkwardly.

"Yeah, well, anyway," said Teddy gruffly, "see ya around."

"Not if I see ya first," growled Woody under his breath.

"What?" snarled Teddy.

"He was joking," said Nat quickly.

Then Teddy Davis laughed. "I guess I deserve it," he said.

"What will you do now?" asked Nat.

"Gonna move away," replied Teddy. "Once I get used to being a werewolf."

After Teddy had gone, Nat sat back on his pillows, exhausted.

"What d'you think of that?" he asked Woody.

"I think," said Woody gravely, "that he'd look better in a pair of Prada shades."

• • •

Dawn. The end of summer, a summer Nat Carver and his family would never forget. After all the parting of the ways, it was time for him and Woody to say good-bye. Still weak, Nat managed to make his way down to Diamond Bay and into the tiny marina, supported by Mick and Jude.

From Iona they had learned that Woody was still of great interest to certain sections of the British government. To save him from ending up like a latter-day Elephant Man, secret, hurried arrangements had been made for Woody to join Evan Carver in Paris as soon as possible. Jude and Apple tearfully kissed Woody good-bye. As he boarded the *Diamond Lil*, Mick hugged him fiercely.

"You look after yourself, son. Remember, it don't matter if you can't find any more Wolven over there" — he nodded toward the continent — "you've got a family here, if you want us."

Woody hugged Mick back. "Thanks, Mick. I want you, whether I find them or not."

Nat and Woody shook hands awkwardly.

"I owe you one," said Nat.

"What do you mean?" asked Woody.

"I saved your life once, you saved mine twice." Nat grinned. "I owe you one."

There was a pause as Woody seemed to be struggling with something to say. Then he grinned back. "Why the big pause?" He laughed. "See, I geddit!"

There seemed so much more that Nat wanted to say, but the *Diamond Lil* bobbed impatiently on the little quay, ready to ride the tide to Le Havre, where they would be met by Evan. Nat watched in silence as his friend vaulted easily into the small vessel, joining Ophelia at the cramped helm.

As Ophelia Tate guided the *Diamond Lil* out of the bay, the early morning sun cast its warming rays of golden light against the quartz-encrusted rocks. For a second, despite Woody's increasing ability to control his changes, Nat saw his friend how he had come to know him best, as a magnificent white Wolven, eyes flashing, standing proud at the stern of the *Diamond Lil*.

Weirdo?

Nat's senses sideslipped into confusion for a second; it was like a radio being tuned inside his brain. Then he grinned in delight. He could hear Woody. As plain as if he were standing right next to him! He could do the two-way thing!

What? He cast his thoughts out across the water to Woody.

Were you the freak or the weirdo? Woody sent back across the waves.

You were the freak! replied Nat.

So that makes you *the weirdo! See you in Paris, brother!*

Nat Carver watched as the boat bobbed merrily around Diamond Bay and slipped out of sight.

ACKNOWLEDGMENTS

Huge thanks go to all the little chickens and the big rooster at the brilliant Chicken House, and to Pat White, Mohsen Shah, and Claire Wilson from RCW.

Thanks to Anna Trenter for your wise editing input and to Hannah Watkinson for reading it first and asking for more.

To Anita Milkins — sorry about Agent Redican!

And finally to Phil, Dan, and Frankie, the real good guys.

Coming Soon!

After dodging mutant werewolves and mad scientists all summer, Nat and Woody have joined the Twilight Circus of Illusion, hoping it might bring them closer to any surviving members of Woody's long lost Wolven clan. But instead, the boys encounter a batty batch of evil in the form of a black widow vampire and her horrifying hive!

CHAPTER 1

PANIC ON THE PLATFORM

Nat Carver was genius at keeping secrets.

He knew that seeing or feeling stuff before it happened was called *precognition*. And it usually meant that something *bad* was going to happen. Nat and his mum, Jude, were waiting impatiently on the platform for the London-to-Paris Eurostar train when his pulse started to race and he only just managed to control the urge to pant like a wolf. He had felt crazy jumpy ever since leaving Temple Gurney, but had told himself it was just excitement at the thought of seeing his dad and Woody again.

He glanced at his mum and couldn't help wincing at her appearance. Yesterday Jude Carver had undergone a complete transformation. Her long brown hair had been bleached blonde and rolled into dreads. Her dark blue eyes were now emerald green, courtesy of some colored contact lenses, and were framed with unflattering wire-rimmed glasses. Worst of all were the slightly protruding false teeth fixed over her own, which Nat thought made her look a bit like a llama or a slightly insane English teacher. Lady Iona de Gourney, their great friend and ally during the whole Proteus saga, had been responsible for Jude's makeover. She had provided them both with sanctuary until Nat had recovered enough to travel, as well as procured the cleverly forged documents they carried, giving both Nat and Jude brand-new identities.

Nat was thankful he had escaped his own extreme makeover. Over the past few months he had grown taller — his muscles had filled out and he'd grown his hair longer. He was barely recognizable as the puny kid of the past summer.

It was freezing, and due to the recent power strikes, the St. Pancras train station was in near darkness. Nat felt the hairs rise up on the back of his neck like hackles. *Why is it*, he thought, *that you only have a premonition when things are going to go wrong?* He scanned the busy platform. It seemed to Nat that *everyone* on it had bad BO. He could see the vapors rising from people and hovering above them like a sort of stanky aura, making him feel as if he was about to lose his breakfast. He tried to concentrate on finding what could be alarming him, but he had brain freeze from overhearing so many snippets of other people's thoughts and conversations. Sifting through all the psychic white noise to zone in on the source took all of Nat's concentration. It was like when you pat yourself on the head with one hand and make circular movements on your stomach with the other: It's impossible to do both things at the same time unless you practice for about three hours every day. Nat couldn't wait to ask Woody how *he* managed to cope with all the extra information.

In the months following the werewolf attack that had almost killed her son, Jude had watched Nat carefully. She had heaved a sigh of relief when the first new moon passed and her only child hadn't shown any signs of sprouting fur and turning into a slavering wolf. When the second new moon came and went, she allowed herself to relax, thanking her lucky stars that whatever gifts Nat may have acquired from Woody's Wolven blood, they didn't include shape-shifting.

Nat was also thankful, not least because he had watched Woody's struggle with his own shape-shifting.

He had seen up close and personal how uncomfortable, not to mention stomach-churningly weird, stretching out of shape could be. But once Nat had realized how thrilled his mum was when there were no physical changes in the weeks after his emergency blood trans-fusion, he decided to keep what was *really* going on to himself. His physical recovery following Lucas Scale's attack had been incredibly fast thanks to the new blood . . . but the recurring nightmares had left scars on his soul.

Since the summer, Nat had developed some seriously cool improvements to his human senses, and had so far managed to keep them secret. The cool things were:

- Long-range, high-frequency hearing
- Sixth sense (needed a bit more practice)
- Telepathy, also known as the two-way mind-meld thing (ditto)
- Super-enhanced infrared vision

His eyesight was *awesome*. Nat had needed glasses for school before all the bother at Helleborine Halt; now he could see for miles and, even more amazing, *he could see in the dark*!

But there was a flip side. Nat struggled with self-control, sometimes resenting his new senses as they threatened to take over. Other problems were:

- Occasional dog breath and increased flatulence (the latter more difficult to keep secret)
- Overdeveloped olfactory glands (which made all smells stronger: see above)
- Other people's nasty, dark thoughts (which he really would rather not know)
- The eye thing

Their train was due to leave in a few minutes and Nat was still sensing that something bad was going to happen. More people spilled onto the already crowded platform, some impatiently pushing and shoving. Nat positioned himself between his mum and the platform edge, worried that the crowd was going to push too much and someone would fall onto the tracks. He hoped like crazy that *that* wasn't going to be the bad thing. Then someone shoved past him, causing the crowd to scatter. In the confusion, Nat heard a scream, and he caught the flash of a steel blade as a knife slashed through the leather strap of an elderly woman's bulging handbag. The woman was knocked to the ground, lost in the melee of people struggling to get out of the way of the knife-wielding thief.

Nat's sight locked onto the slightly built figure running away. He was dressed in black, his hood pulled over his head, a scarf covering most of his face. Nat's body was overtaken by an overwhelming urge to make chase. He could feel his heart pumping Wolven blood, preparing his muscles for fight *and* flight. He wanted to *chase*, to run him down; not because the thief had committed a nasty, cowardly crime, but because Nat *needed* to, as though an ON switch had been flicked in his brain. He shoved his way through the crowd and was off on his toes. He could hear his mum screaming for him to stop, but he ignored her and honed in on the hoodie, who by now was near the terminal, glancing over his shoulder to see if he was being followed. When he spotted Nat gaining on him, he sped up, and Nat could smell his fear as he closed in. As he ran, he realized there was a strange noise coming from his throat. *He was growling!* It both excited and frightened him.

He launched himself at the hoodie, knocking him to the ground with a muffled *whump* and wrenching the bag from him. Nat pulled the scarf away from his face. *The thief was a girl!* She stared up at him, panting hard.

"Your eyes!" she said breathlessly.

"What?" snarled Nat.

"Your *eyes* . . . ," she repeated.

Nat sprang to his feet. Other people, including his mum, had joined in the chase and were fast approaching. He examined the backs of his hands as though expecting to see them covered with fur. They weren't. He willed his pulse to slow and his muscles to relax. He glared down at the girl.

"What *about* my eyes?" he demanded.

"They . . . they changed . . . they were *golden*," she gasped.

"And now?" growled Nat.

"N-normal!" she stammered, shocked. "Blue. But when you took me down, they changed."

"You better get out of here," said Nat. The last thing he wanted was to get involved. If the police were called and he was a witness, it could lead to all sorts of unwelcome attention. Luckily, the hoodie didn't need to be told twice. Nat watched her speed off into the afternoon gloom.

CHAPTER 2

THINGS ARE GETTING HAIRY

Nat and Jude Carver were happily unaware that their plans to leave England had already been discovered. A few days before they left the southwest countryside for London, certain information regarding their whereabouts had been passed on to a man named Quentin Crone, the former head of Her Majesty's Military Intelligence, otherwise known as MI5, the British Secret Service.

At a clandestine location in London not far from Fleet Street, Quentin Crone was sitting in his new office, trying hard not to think about the night he had first heard Nat Carver's name. Sighing deeply, he gazed around his new place of work with something like dread. Although it wasn't yet three o'clock in the afternoon, the narrow street was dark and eerily deserted. The only light inside was from the embers of the fire and the glow of Crone's computer screen. The rest of the vast room was murky, with shadows in every corner.

Crone glanced nervously around him, as he so often did these days, half expecting to see something lurking behind him, hidden in the gloom: a nightmare creature that slavered and snarled, its eyes glowing with violence and hunger.

Stop thinking about it! he told himself sternly. Unfortunately his brain had other ideas. Awake or asleep, Crone was both haunted and taunted by images of creatures that he had believed only existed in the most lurid of horror movies.

The night his world had turned upside down — when he had no choice but to believe that monsters were real — was tattooed on his brain forever. Quentin Crone had seen things he had never thought possible. *Werewolves!* Great big black ones, ten feet tall, loping toward him, *coming for him*, thick ropes of drool swinging rhythmically, almost hypnotically, from their impossible-looking bloody jaws.

At a remote stately home in deepest, darkest Somerset, experiments to create the ultimate fighting machine for the twenty-first century had gone badly wrong. Barking-mad scientist Dr. Gabriel Gruber had tried to fuse the DNA of crazed werewolves with that of a telepathic Wolven — a noble shape-shifting creature thought (until recently) to exist in legend only. *And the government had known all about it!* Quentin Crone had felt he had no alternative but to resign as soon as he had been decommissioned. Two good things had come out of it, though: The crooked prime minister and his entire corrupt cabinet had all been fired; and, even better — a warm smile lit Crone's tired face whenever he thought of it — the boy, Nat Carver, and the shape-shifting Wolven creature had *escaped*!

His appointment as Head of NightShift had followed shortly after, and Crone had hit the ground running. He hadn't even had time to take off his coat on his first day before he had been called out to investigate a nasty poltergeist infestation in Putney.

Not for the first time, Crone wondered what the devil he had been thinking of by accepting the appointment in the first place. He had never even heard of NightShift, for a start, until he had been contacted by an old colleague, a Professor Robert Paxton. According to the professor, the covert agency code-named NightShift had been operating for a number of years, quietly exterminating evil beings or forces without too many humans getting shredded.

The professor had shown Crone disturbing new evidence that supernatural events were on the rise, the threat to humans from malignant forces was now greater than global warming, and vampires and werewolves had overtaken human terrorist activity. In light of recent events (and an unexpected vacancy), Professor Paxton had convinced Quentin Crone he was just the man for the job. An unheated office in Middle Temple Lane was the NightShift headquarters, where Crone was to spend his days and nights making lethal decisions, drinking tea, and counting the dead bodies.

BBBBRRRRRRZZZZZZ!

Crone's heart almost leaped up into his throat as the old-fashioned intercom on his desk made him jump.

For heaven's sake, man, get a grip, he told himself sternly. "Yes?" he rasped, sounding more bad-tempered than he felt.

"Cuppa tea, boss?" a bright female voice crackled through to his office.

"I'm awash with the stuff, Fish," he groaned, his voice sounding echoey and insubstantial in the cavernous room, "but if you're making hot chocolate with sprinkles and marshmallows, I'd be glad of some company."

There was a knack to opening the heavy, studded door to his office, and Crone waited patiently until the sounds of someone grappling with the handle stopped. A slightly built girl tottered across the ancient carpet on the highest, shiniest pair of platform shoes that Crone had ever seen, plonked a tray with two steaming mugs onto his desk, and arranged her skinny body in the chair opposite him.

"*Woohooo*, you're looking a bit rough," blurted Agent Alexandra Fish, studying Crone's features with her beady eyes.

"Not sleeping," said Crone bluntly, distracted by the pile of red files she had also brought with her. Someone had scrawled REALLY REALLY URGENT across the top in thick black marker. "What are those?"

Fish looked down at the folders she'd carried in as though she was surprised they were there. "Oh . . . uh, more cases, boss."

Crone groaned and leaned forward again, pinching the bridge of his nose between his thumb and forefinger. Fish had only known Quentin Crone for a few days, but she could see how worry and tiredness had drawn lines onto his craggy face. She fervently hoped he wasn't going to quit on them, or worse. Dear old Freddie Alton, the last head of NightShift, had cracked under the incredible pressure of running the agency. The last Fish had heard was that poor Freddie was currently in a high-security facility for the chronically insane, locked in a windowless room with walls made of mattresses, wearing a very tight jacket with lots of buckles and no armholes.

"We have more cases than we have agents," said Crone wearily, gesturing to the pile of red files.

Not much gets past this guy, thought Fish, impressed. Since she had joined NightShift, there had been a worrying increase in werewolf goings-on, not to mention vampire activity and the number of people affected by demonic possessions and hauntings.

"So, like, things are getting hairy" — she grinned — "if you'll pardon the pun."

At last Crone smiled, his tired eyes crinkling at the corners. "We're learning all the time," he said, "but, as you know from experience, we're only human."

"Obviously," said Fish in surprise. There was something

in Crone's voice that made her look at him more closely from behind her glasses. "What are you getting at?" she queried.

"Well . . . do you not think that perhaps we are at a disadvantage?" asked Crone.

"Huh?" Fish mumbled.

"We're only *human*," he stressed. "Humans investigating supernatural and paranormal activities. Not exactly a fair fight, is it?"

"We do OK." Fish frowned, still not sure what her new boss was going on about. "And NightShift is growing. We've got ten fully trained agents and two trainees."

"Remind me again why NightShift was formed," said Crone, steepling his fingers.

Fish gave him a quizzical look, kicked off her unfeasible platform shoes, and curled up her stockinged feet underneath her.

"To kill monsters," she said.

Crone grinned.

"These are dark days, Fish. The events in Somerset last summer, proving that werewolves really do exist, meant I had to ask myself a very important question."

"Like, if werewolves really exist, what *else* is real?" Alex Fish said solemnly.

Crone nodded. "And NightShift answered those questions for me. Investigating the paranormal has always been seen as a bit of a joke for those not in the know."

"If the public knew what *really* happened . . . ," began Fish. "Like, if they knew what was *down there* . . ."

Both Crone and Fish allowed their gaze to slide toward the floor. Underneath the faded red-and-gold carpet that covered the mammoth room was a giant trapdoor. If opened, it would reveal seventy-seven steps, each one painstakingly hand-cut into the granite many centuries before. The catacombs beneath were stuffed with more fabulous secrets and priceless artifacts than those allegedly held in the Vatican and Area 51 put together. Crone allowed himself a small shudder whenever he stopped to think about the strange and often terrible things stored *down there . . . in the dark . . .*